Too Late For Regrets

by

Maureen Jabour

Too Late for Regrets by Maureen Jabour

Published by
Montana Moon Productions, LLC
1158 26th St.
PMB #519
Santa Monica, CA 90403

This is a work of fiction. All characters, organizations, and events portrayed in this novel are products of the author's imagination.

ISBN 0692229663

Thanks to Genesse Carrillo
Writer's Assistant, Montana Moon Productions

Cover designed by Ruan Jacobs
The Freshman Graphic Design

Dedication

This book is dedicated to the men and women of law enforcement throughout the United States. Also to our first responders and fire fighters.

They have chosen careers which sometimes involve them in difficult and dangerous situations.

Also

To my husband, Chris Jabour

Acknowledgements

My son, Dr. Bradley A. Jabour

Nicole Chidrawi, Montana Moon Productions, Santa Monica, California

Police Detective, John Routa

Gentle Readers: Pat Routa, Jan Keller

About the Author

Maureen Jabour emigrated from South Africa to the United States with her family in 1979. In South Africa, several of her short stories were published in P.E.N. New South African Writing.

She was gardening editor for Colorado Homes and Lifestyles magazine for several years. Her gardening books, *Celebrating a Small English Garden*, *A Medley of Gardens*, and *Magical Gardens* were on the local best seller list for many weeks. *Celebrating a Small English Garden* was a finalist in the Colorado Center for the Book Award.

For twenty years there were tours of her garden followed by an English tea. These tours benefited the National Kidney Foundation, and the Women's Library Association, which raises money for the University of Denver's Penrose Library.

She lives with her husband in Golden, Colorado.

Part One
Elizabeth - An Exceptional Woman

The Scent of Lavender

Gentle Reader: This is a tale of a love affair between a beautiful South African woman of Scottish heritage who had emigrated to the U.S. several years before these events took place and a brave, handsome police officer. On their first meeting, her dormant passions were aroused. His good looks and gentle charm had enabled him to conquer many women, though none of these conquests had ever touched his heart. Now he was to meet a woman with whom for the first time he was to fall in love; a love so deep it would change his life forever. This unlikely duo was to embark on a rapturous journey which would end in disappointment, disloyalty and bitter regret.

Living in different worlds they never would have met had it not been for a minor accident and a small boy on a bicycle. Shall we call it Kismet? So turn off your cell phone, ignore any text messages, settle down in a comfortable chair, and, to paraphrase Bette Davis in the movie, *All About Eve*, "Fasten your seatbelts, it's going to be an interesting, exciting and bumpy ride."

Chapter One

Elizabeth Murray walked down the street of her neighborhood observing the pretty gardens along her route. Having moved in recently she hadn't had time to explore her new surroundings. Lots of tulips, she noted, and her favorite ground-covers, brilliantly colored basket-of-gold and deep pink creeping phlox which would make a splendid show later in the month. A border of pinks (dianthus) was especially striking; these, she thought, could be incorporated into her own new bed. The houses were well built and architecturally conservative. She knew she would be happy here.

A mile into her walk brought her to the main road with its four-way stop. This was the end of her neighborhood. Adjusting her straw hat, she crossed into a different area of solid brick houses which had been built, she had been told, in the late 1940's for returning World War II servicemen. They were ranch style houses with two windows on either side of the doors. There was obvious pride of ownership here as evidenced by the neatly trimmed hedges and lawns. The freshly painted doors with their gleaming brass knockers added to this impression.

Another mile brought her to a shallow stream. She turned into the cul-de-sac and ahead of her saw a wooden bridge which led into a wooded area. She hesitated; the bridge was narrow and looked unstable. She felt hot and tired. She turned around and in so doing caught her foot in a small pothole. She crashed to the ground, her leg twisting under her. She gasped with pain as she tried to move her leg. There wasn't a soul in sight, for in this isolated spot there was no traffic. She could feel sweat trickling down her face. She started to panic. Who would see her? She might have to be here for hours. Her hat had been knocked forward, but under the brim, she saw coming out of the alley a small boy on a bicycle. He dismounted and ran towards her.

"Ma'am, you've hurt yourself, your leg's bleeding."

She smiled weakly.

"I'm so pleased to see you. Do you think you could get someone to help me?"

"Yes," he said, "I'll get our neighbor, he always helps people."

He got on his bike and pedaled away, turning into a side street.

"Sir," he called to a man who was about to get into his car, "a pretty lady has fallen down around the corner and she's bleeding."

The man backed the car out, then followed the boy into the cul-de-sac. At the sight of her his heart lurched—his dream woman. For the past month he'd seen her working in her garden. Jesus, and now he was actually going to touch her? She was facing away from him, her hat tilted forward.

"Thank God," she said, "I was getting desperate. Please lift me up, my elbow is killing me."

He put his hands under her armpits, lifting her so that she was able to sit up.

"Could you straighten my leg, I think I've twisted my ankle."

He lifted her leg, then cupped her foot in his hand; so soft, he thought, like a small child's.

"Does it hurt when I move it up and down?"

"No, not too much."

"Can you wriggle your toes?"

She wriggled them then giggled.

"I could probably play this little piggy went to market."

He laughed.

"I don't think we'll have time for that. I'm going to move your foot from side to side, does that hurt?"

She winced.

"That's so sore! Do you think something's broken?"

"Well, I'm not an expert, but it seems it's very bruised and there's swelling."

He stood up.

"I've got a first aid kit in my car, now don't run away."

She laughed.

"You're so funny."

She took off her hat and looked up at him.

"Good Lord, you're a police officer."

"Yes Ma'am, Captain Timothy Bennet, ready to serve and protect."

"Well, could you start serving and protecting right now by please getting me some water. I'm dying of thirst, and I might end up just being a pile of whitened bones."

He grinned.

"They'll certainly be attractive bones. Daniel, stop staring at the lady and get a bottle of water, it's on the back seat."

Daniel continued staring.

"She's such a pretty lady, only she talks funny."

They both laughed.

"Daniel, I'm going to talk funny again to say thank you for fetching this gentleman to help me," Elizabeth said.

"You're welcome Ma'am."

Timothy uncapped the bottle and she gulped it down until she'd finished almost half.

"That's enough," he took the bottle from her. "You'll make yourself sick if you drink too much."

He took out the first aid kit from his trunk. Then he knelt beside her. She looked at him and thought what a handsome man, brown almost black straight hair, interesting eyebrows, slightly narrow brown eyes, a strong nose and a mouth, well, she had to admit it was a nice mouth. And here I am looking like a ragamuffin, old skirt, disreputable straw hat and string tying my hair back.

"I'm afraid sitting here like this I must look like a homeless person. All I need is a small dog and a placard saying 'WILL WORK FOR FOOD.'"

He was amused.

"With no traffic here I doubt whether you'd collect much money, but I must say you do improve the look of this cul-de-sac."

He couldn't resist sneaking a look at her. Christ, the face of an angel, the most captivating face he'd ever seen. It reminded him of that model Carol something or other that he always looked for in the men's magazines. Light brown slightly wavy hair tied back with—was that string? Blue eyes that were so trusting and innocent, and two dimples in her cheeks. When he looked at her mouth he thought, keep calm, Timothy, don't look at that mouth again.

He took out a bottle, uncapped it and said, "This is sterile water; I'll clean up that scrape. The bleeding makes it look worse than it really is. And this is hydrogen peroxide which will prevent infection. It's going to sting a bit."

She winced.

"Sorry about that, but it is effective. I'll cover it with a large Band-Aid that should stop the bleeding," Timothy said.

He took out a bandage and starting at her instep wound it around and over her ankle several times. His hands were shaking slightly, damn, he was as nervous as a schoolboy.

She contemplated his neck, really nice, and what a lovely haircut.

Really, she chided herself, what other hairstyle would a police officer have? Dreadlocks? A ponytail?

He stood up.

"That should do it."

They smiled at each other.

The best looking man in Hamilton City, she lamented to herself, why hadn't she at least worn a respectable hat?

She touched her cheek.

"You've got a smudge of dirt on the side of your face, let me wipe it off," Timothy said.

He bent over her and cleaned the dirt off with a strip of wet gauze.

"While I'm about it, I'll wipe the sweat off your forehead. There, you're as good as new. Let me help you up."

She stood on one foot and looking at the side of the cruiser said, "Why, you're a sheriff, our sheriff?"

"Well, Mrs. Murray, I'm relieved to see that a South African can still read English."

She stared at him in amazement.

"I'm astounded, how do you know my name and where I'm from?"

"It's a long story," he said, "can you put your foot down?"

He opened the passenger side door.

"I'll have to help you."

He swept her up into his arms. A subtle flowery perfume made his head swim.

"Comfortable?" he asked as he seated her. "Here's your hat, shoe, and most important your piece of string."

When he was settled behind the wheel, she said, "So what's the long story?"

He took a deep breath.

"A month ago as I was coming home I saw you digging in that front bed. It was unusual to see a woman digging in your upscale neighborhood. People there have teams of workers to do that sort of thing. I saw you dragging bags of compost. I stopped for five minutes and watched as you emptied half the bag into a bucket. You spread that around, then you picked up the bag and emptied that onto the bed."

"That's because women should never carry heavy bags, it's bad for the back. Besides dragging bags is good for the leg muscles," Elizabeth said.

He looked down at her legs.

"I can see that, and if ever I come across other women gardeners I'll certainly pass on that information."

He continued, "A few days later at lunch time I saw a Botanic Gardens truck in your driveway, and you were showing two men where to plant a tree, it's a great tree."

"Yes, it's a lovely tree; flowering pear—'Chanticleer'— and," she added, "you certainly are observant."

"I'm trained to be observant, and I must warn you not to leave your garage doors open, there are a lot of bad guys around."

"Thank you for that tip, but you still haven't told me how you know so much about me."

"My neighbor is a keen gardener. She often walks in your area. She got talking to you, and you told her you were an immigrant from South Africa, you're a widow with a small son. She was the one who gave all that information."

"But why did you want to know about me?"

He hesitated.

"Because Mrs. Murray, I'd become uh, very interested in you," he paused, "more interested than was good for me. I never dreamed I'd ever meet you, it's sort of like fate."

She said, "Call it Kismet."

He looked puzzled.

"Who's he?"

"Never mind, and I'm sure you have work to do, perhaps you should take me home now."

He sighed, "Yes, I can't be late for my shift."

Daniel ran up as he started the car, "Captain, will you turn your siren on?"

"No Daniel," he grinned, "unless Mrs. Murray wants me to."

She cringed.

"For Pete's sake, don't do that, I'm embarrassed enough as it is."

They arrived at her house and he came around to open the door for her. He helped her out and said, "I don't think you'll be able to hop up those six steps."

Once more she was swept up into his arms—oh God, he thought, I wish there were a hundred steps—and again she was staring at that really nice haircut.

"Where's your key?"

"Under that pot."

He sighed.

"Mrs. Murray, that's the first place an intruder would look. Thread some string through the key and hang it around your neck. Always lock your door when you're working in the garden."

"Thank you, that's a good idea. Isn't string useful? Gardeners should always keep a ball of string handy."

"I'll remember that when I'm in my garden," he said solemnly.

He opened the door and she said, "I'm so grateful for your help. What would I have done without you? Also for all your tips and information. Tell me, how can I ever thank you?"

He hesitated, saying to himself, go on Timothy, ask her, you'll never have another opportunity. He took a deep breath, here goes, "You can thank me by having coffee with me."

She also hesitated.

[Gentle Reader: We have reached the pivotal point in this tale. If she says "no" this narrative will come to a screeching halt. However, if she says...]

"Yes, I'd love to have coffee with you. I'd really like to see you again."

Whew, he breathed a sigh of relief, his gamble had paid off.

"Mrs. Murray, I'll be away for a week on a training course. Can I call you when I get back?"

"Please do, my telephone number is in the book," she said.

"It was a pleasure meeting you Mrs. Murray."

She smiled up at him.

"We needn't be so formal, why don't you call me Elizabeth, and if I may, I'll call you Timothy? After all, we're not in a Jane Austen novel."

"Who? Jane who?"

"Never mind."

She hopped into the house, then into the kitchen. She switched on the kettle. What she needed was a nice hot cup of tea.

Meanwhile, Timothy pondered on the unexpected delight of meeting Elizabeth, and the expectation of seeing her again at their coffee date. His thoughts turned to the shift ahead of him—the usual assholes fighting outside a bar, some other son-of-a-bitch beating his wife and children, and probably a few high-speed chases to catch drunks weaving in and out of the traffic. He put in his favorite country music tape and hummed along with Johnny Cash. What luck to have met this woman he'd become obsessed with, and what a weird way she had of talking. And who the hell were Kismet and Jane something or other? She was definitely different from any other woman he'd ever met. Her confidence, lack of guile, her sense of humor and her striking beauty were what he found captivating.

To think that in a week's time he'd be sitting opposite that gorgeous creature gazing at her exquisite face, listening to her talk in that English accent with its slight twang, inhaling again that faint light fragrance that seemed part of her allure. Maybe he'd even get to hold her hand? He shook his head in disbelief. Here he was dreaming about holding a woman's hand, when usually an hour after meeting a new woman he'd be well on the way to another conquest. His radio was crackling. He switched off the tape. Shit, another holdup at a bank. He activated his siren, turned on his flashing lights, brooding as he raced along the highway towards what would be several hours of mayhem, thinking of the increase in armed robberies due, it was said, to the economic downturn. Combined with the influx of gangs from Los Angeles, the resources of Law Enforcement were being stretched to their limits.

Adding to his worries, one of his best officers had been placed on administrative leave, accused of using "excessive force" in a confrontation with two armed men. Crap, out would come the usual marchers, rallying, carrying placards, "Stop Police

Brutality." The city would descend into chaos if it wasn't for its dedicated men and women.

His muscles tensed as he reached his assembled team.

"Three blocks down, Captain, 1st National Bank."

Their sirens wailed; like the Red Sea parting before the Israelites, the traffic in front of them miraculously divided allowing them safe passage. Just one more "incident" which would probably end in gunfire. The important thing was to keep his team safe.

That night as Elizabeth prepared for bed, she thought, how sweet and gentle he was and a lovely sense of humor, the only man, she felt in many years who had caused her heart to beat faster. She hummed an old tune, one that her parents had danced to. She and her sister had watched their parents and their friends dancing to that music, big band music. What fun those parties were, and when she heard that music, it filled her with nostalgia.

Composing herself for sleep she continued humming.

And come to think of it, that was a really nice haircut.

Chapter Two

The Coffee Break

[Gentle Reader: You will become aware that Elizabeth has an inexhaustible supply of stories; she is widely read, and has an infinite capacity for soaking up information which she is happy to impart to all listeners. She is a raconteuse, her active brain switches from one subject to another with alarming speed. World events, historical and literary allusions, jokes and recipes. This flood of information, as we will see, can bewilder the listener.]

The phone rang. She answered on the second ring.
"Hello."
"Elizabeth, it's Timothy, how's your ankle?"
"Much better, thanks to you. Another week and it'll be back to normal."
"So are we meeting for coffee?" He held his breath.
"Of course, I'm looking forward to it. I thought we'd meet at Wholesome Products. There's a coffee shop there and as I have to get a few groceries I could meet you at say 11:00a.m."
"Great," he said, "I can't wait to see you."
He got there at 10:30a.m., not wanting to miss a minute of seeing her parking her little yellow car, then watching her coming into the shop. He was nervous, wiping his hands several times on a paper napkin. He saw her swing into a parking space and then as she approached the glass doors pushing a cart, several men leapt up to help her. She looked stunning; a white skirt brushing her knees, a white and blue striped T shirt tightly belted, her hair combed away from her face and falling in slight waves to her shoulders. He watched her walking up and down the aisles, and then she was

13

standing in front of him, her smile radiant. His mouth felt dry. What sort of conversation could he possibly have with her? He needn't have worried; she had enough conversation for a dozen people. He watched fascinated as she took a sip of coffee and a bite of her cookie, her pink tongue licking her lips, her eyes looking at him speculatively. He was so intent in his inspection of her that he missed the first part of what she was saying.

"...so I couldn't decide whether to plant the pink or the white petunias. White shows up so well at dusk, but on the other hand I do love that deep pink shade, they're so vibrant, don't you agree?"

Huh? What was she talking about?

"So," she took another sip of coffee. "I decided to think about it some more and went inside to make some meringues."

He tried to concentrate.

"Meringues? What's that?"

"They're those white confections you buy in the pastry section, but I must warn you, don't buy them. They're baked so hard, they're like concrete, you could break a tooth on them." She giggled, "I've known people who actually used a jackhammer to break them."

He promised not to buy them, whatever meringues were.

"So," she said, "I decided to make a big batch, they're my son's favorite dessert. I separated six eggs being careful not to let any yolks into the bowl, because if you do the whites won't beat up stiffly, and then you have to start all over again."

"Okay," he said, "I'll remember that, no yolks."

"Then you add sugar one tablespoon at a time and continue beating. But," she warned, "if you add too much sugar at one time, the mixture won't get stiff."

"Right," he said, humoring her, "got that, no yolks, not too much sugar at one time."

"Okay, now it's stiff, you put a spoonful of the mixture onto a cookie sheet or tinfoil, then put it in the oven at 250^0 for about two hours. You see," she said earnestly, "they don't really bake, they sort of dry out, and served with strawberries and cream, they're scrumptious."

"Oh Lord," she said suddenly, "I think I forgot to turn on the oven, and it's starting to drizzle, I must go."

"Oh please," he begged, "don't go yet, whatever those things are, they can't burn if the oven's off, and the rain will hold off for a while."

"Well alright," she said, "I could tell you some more about those petunias..."

He stopped listening. He was dreaming; he was holding her in his arms, his face buried in her neck, inhaling that faint perfume, his hands starting to move up, they were cupping her firm...

"Well boyo," said a loud voice, interrupting his blissful reverie, "this looks cozy."

Shit, it was that loudmouth John, his Deputy Sheriff.

"Hello John," he said unenthusiastically.

"So what's going on? I can't stay long, my radio's going crazy. There's been a cloudburst over the Northern suburbs, all those underpasses will be flooding. Well seeing you aren't inviting me to sit down, I'll invite myself."

He took a gulp of coffee then turned to look at Elizabeth.

"Wow," he said, ogling her, "I haven't seen you around."

"I only recently moved into the area."

"John, this is Mrs. Murray," Timothy was annoyed at the interruption, "Mrs. Murray, this is my Deputy Sheriff, Lieutenant John O'Donell. He's Irish. He's got the gift of the gab."

"And a lot of other gifts as well." He grinned cheekily at her.

"John," Timothy reprimanded him, "none of that coarse talk in front of this lady."

But she was laughing; another good looking officer. Where was the city recruiting their officers from? Hollywood?

"Hello," she said as he took both her hands in his.

"Wow," he said again.

"You've already said that twice," Timothy was irritable, "and you can give her hands back now. Mrs. Murray is from South Africa," he added.

"South Africa, I wouldn't mind meeting fifty South Africans if they look like you."

He took a sip of coffee.

"So where did you two meet?"

"The gallant captain helped me when I fell down in the street," she said.

"Huh, he's got all the luck. If it was me I'd probably be helping some old bag with varicose veins."

She was laughing when another voice interrupted them.

"Well Timothy, where the hell have you been?"

Oh crap, he groaned inwardly, that nuisance, Jean.

"I think," she said accusingly, "we have some unfinished business."

She leaned against the table, her uniform pants stretched snugly over her shapely buttocks. Every stitch was doing its duty.

What an attractive girl, thought Elizabeth. Blonde hair drawn back in a bun, light blue eyes that were looking imploringly at Timothy. Lovely figure, too. Why was he treating her so coolly?

John intervened tactfully.

"Mrs. Murray, this is Sergeant Jean Sedecki. Mrs. Murray is from South Africa," he added.

She looked at Elizabeth.

"South Africa? I'm dying to go to Africa. I want to see all those wild animals, lions, tigers, camels."

Elizabeth said, "Africa is a continent. South Africa is one of fifty countries in Africa. And you won't find camels in South Africa, they're in North Africa."

"There you are, Jean, showing your ignorance again," said John.

"You shut up, John," Jean glared at him, "I didn't ask for your opinion."

Elizabeth said diplomatically, "And I must tell you that camels are useful animals. Do you know that Lawrence of Arabia used camels to transport explosives and ammunitions which were used to blow up Turkish trains? This led to the defeat of the Turks in the Great War, but of course you knew all that history?"

They gaped at her and shook their heads. They hadn't known that.

"And," she continued, "Lawrence of Arabia had promised the Arabs that in return for their help in defeating the Turks, the British would guarantee their independence. But of course after the war, Britain reneged on their promise and the Arabs saw their territory divided into Jordan, Syria, Iraq and Lebanon. Isn't that shocking?"

They all agreed; it was shocking.

Timothy's head was in a whirl. How to process all this information, and when would she stop talking?

Jean was tired of hearing about camels defeating someone or other. She turned her attention once more toward Timothy.

"I'm expecting to hear from you."

Elizabeth, wanting to deflect her attention from Timothy, said smoothly, "Sergeant, what's your last name?"

"Sedecki, my grandparents were Polish."

"I knew it," said Elizabeth. "When I saw your wonderful high cheekbones, I said to myself you must be Polish. All the girls in Poland are quite beautiful and they all have your high cheekbones. If you were to visit Poland, you'd fit right in."

"Thank you, Mrs. Murray, I'm thrilled to hear that. It's kind of you to say so."

"And," said Elizabeth, "they're such brave people. During World War II, cavalry officers on their horses with their swords drawn—the officers I mean, not the horses—galloped towards the German tanks which were readying for their attack on Warsaw, and of course they were all mown down by machine gun fire, including the horses. However, many brave Poles made their way to England where they were trained as Spitfire pilots. They were known as the 303 Polish Fighter Squadron, and many of them were decorated for bravery by King George; he was the present Queen's father who ascended the throne after his brother King Edward VII abdicated because of his love for Mrs. Simpson. You've heard of Mrs. Simpson?" she asked not very hopefully.

They shook their heads.

"Never heard of her," they all said.

Timothy feared that she was about to launch into a long story about this Mrs. whatever her name was, so he intervened hastily.

"Never mind her! Finish telling us about Poland."

"Yes," said Jean, "I'm really interested in all this history."

Reluctantly, Elizabeth switched from Mrs. Simpson (such a fascinating woman) and continued her tale of Polish bravery.

"Over a hundred thousand men escaped from Poland and joined up with the Allied forces. With the British army they stormed Monte Cassino in Italy which opened the way for the invasion and liberation of Italy. The British love the Polish people. So you see Sergeant you must visit Poland and connect with your roots. Forget Africa, if you want to see wild animals why not visit the zoo? And," she said with a twinkle in her eye, "if the women there are beautiful, the men aren't bad looking either."

They all laughed.

"Thank you Mrs. Murray, I'll definitely be making a trip there. It was a pleasure meeting you."

Timothy gazed at Elizabeth. What a woman, and where did she get all this information? His head was buzzing with a confused mixture of petunias, pink meringues, no yolks, Polish Arabs, camels attacking who, Mrs. what's-her-name, and the King of Italy?

"Come on Jean," said John, "never mind a trip to Poland, we've got an emergency trip to make to those underpasses. Stop dawdling. Timothy, I know it's your afternoon off, but if you can come and give us a hand."

He winked at Timothy.

"I hope I'll see you again Mrs. Murray."

They both left.

"What a nice man," Elizabeth said, "but rather impudent."

"Oh John's my best friend, he's a great guy, one of the best."

Her hands were on the table. He slid his hands over until their fingertips were touching. She looked thoughtfully at him, then moved her hands away.

"That girl's in love with you," said Elizabeth.

"Well, I'm not in love with her," Timothy said shortly, "she's too aggressive, she's a pain."

"So did you have an, er, intimate encounter with her?"

"You mean did I sleep with her?" he said bluntly. "Yes, a few months ago, but she started working on my nerves, calling, leaving messages, and," he went on indignantly, "she'd wait at my car after my shift, and I was so tired I didn't want to see anyone, let alone undressing and..."

"That's enough Timothy, I don't want to hear any details," said Elizabeth.

"Okay, I won't say any more, I just wanted to be honest with you."

"And I appreciate that. Anyway I liked her, in fact, I admire her. I hope I'll meet her again."

"Admire her? Why?" he asked puzzled.

"Because she has strength of character. Look at the career she has chosen and doing it in a man's world, oh yes, I admire her," said Elizabeth.

"Are you a feminist?" he asked suspiciously.

"No Timothy, I'm not, but that's irrelevant. Give credit where credit is due. You ought to be thankful that there are women who would enter into such a dangerous field, and besides, she has a lovely face, a face that could launch a thousand ships."

Huh, what ships? How did ships get into the conversation?

"You're right, Elizabeth," he said grudgingly, "maybe I'm too harsh with her, because she does do a good job. In fact, I'm giving serious thought to putting her name in for promotion. And what's this about ships?"

Her dimples were out in full force.

"Oh Timothy, I'm so pleased to hear that, and the thousand ships were sent to rescue Helen of Troy, she was so beautiful you see. Paris fell in love with her and kidnapped her..."

"You mean Paris in France?"

"No Timothy, Paris was from Troy in Turkey. Anyway, it's all in the Iliad by Homer..."

"So Troy was gay?" asked Timothy.

She was laughing so much she could hardly speak.

"Now you're mixing me up," she spluttered, "anyway I'll lend you the book someday, although I've read somewhere that it might be a fable; a sort of myth."

"Well a myth is as good as a mile," he said.

She laughed delightedly.

"I don't know what to do with you, you're so clever and you're a scream."

He knew what he wanted to do with her.

"I'm tired of talking about those people, but I'll tell you I don't care how high Jean's cheekbones are, your cheekbones are in a class of their own. And if I was going to rescue you, I'd send a million ships."

"Oh Timothy, I do like you," her eyes sparkled at him, "and listen, we've had so many interruptions and all this talking."

He lifted an eyebrow. He hadn't heard anyone else but her talking.

"So I haven't really had the chance to thank you for your kindness. What I suggest is that I take you to lunch, so that we can really get to know each other. Would you like to have lunch with me on your next day off?"

What a question. Would he like to have lunch with her? Was the Pope a Catholic?

"It's a casual restaurant, salads and sandwiches, that sort of thing. But I don't recommend the lettuce salad. I suspect they use that nasty bottled dressing, and you know dressing is so easy to make. Olive oil, vinegar or lemon juice, a soupçon of mustard, a teaspoon of sugar, mix well and it's a really palatable dressing, not like that industrial strength glue that passes for dressing."

He was baffled. Soupçon? Palatable? What was she talking about now?

"What's soupçon again?"

"It's French for a little bit. Soupçon sounds more interesting, don't you agree?"

He agreed, loving the earnestness of her pronouncements.

"So we'll have a nice intimate lunch and then we can talk."

He doubted that he'd be doing the talking, but he wouldn't mind. She could recite the whole of the Gettysburg Address, three Hail Marys, and the entire Rosary, just as long as he could sit opposite her and feast his eyes on her entrancing face, and watch those dimples appear and disappear. Maybe she'd even let him hold her hand and a little bit more?

"I think I'll go now, the rain seems to be stopping."

"Elizabeth, I'm worried about you in your little car. Avoid your usual route, don't go anywhere near the underpasses or the highway. Promise me you'll use the route past the University."

She nodded gratefully at him.

"I promise."

He picked up her shopping bag and with his other arm around her waist, they ran to her car. He opened the door, put the bag in, then as she stood gazing up at him the temptation to hold her was too great. He lifted her up slightly and brought his mouth down on hers. It was a soft kiss, he didn't want to alarm her.

"I can taste cinnamon," he said.

"Well if I'd known I was going to be kissed I wouldn't have eaten that cookie. You should have warned me."

He hugged her.

"I love the taste of cinnamon, especially when I can taste it on your lips."

"I'm glad to hear that, because I make a delicious cake with quite a lot of cinnamon."

Christ, he thought, another recipe. He lifted her up again and silenced her with a firmer kiss just as she was saying, "You sift…"

This cut off the recipe which to him sounded like a cup of baking powder and a teaspoon of flour.

"Well, um, yes."

For the first time that day she was speechless.

"I'll go now."

The rain was pelting down as he ran to his SUV. He activated his siren and turned on the revolving light on the roof. On his way he saw her turning left, the long route past the University. That stupid little car with its lawn mower wheels. Suppose she got stuck? He could picture the car filling up with water. It could tilt over. She wouldn't be able to open the doors. Oh God, Elizabeth could drown! He tried to concentrate as he reached the first underpass. The teams were pulling cars out using tow ropes. He worked frantically for half an hour, then his worry over Elizabeth became too much for him.

"I'm going to the next underpass," he shouted to John and Jean, who were directing traffic.

He drove through what had now become rivers, his huge wheels easily fording the water lapping around them. He stopped outside her house and saw with alarm that no lights were on. He ran to the door and pounded on it.

"Elizabeth! Elizabeth!"

She had arrived five minutes earlier. She had taken off her damp clothes and had put on a robe when she heard the hammering on the door.

"Who is it?"

"It's Timothy."

She fell into his arms.

"Oh Timothy, I was so scared, I got stuck just past the University, and when I opened the door I saw the water was past the tires."

She was trembling.

"A man in a big car like yours pushed me out."

"There, there my darling," he hugged her, "I was so worried about you, I had to see if you were safe."

His hands were under her robe, the feel of her silky skin made his head spin. His hands were moving up and were cupping her firm...

"No Timothy," she pushed him away, "don't do that."

"Oh God," he groaned, "I'm sorry, please forgive me, I lost my head."

He kissed her forehead, the tip of her nose, "Forgive me? I've got to go."

As the door banged shut behind him, she sat down. She was trembling, but this time not from fright but from the knowledge that she had almost lost her head. She felt that she might lose control of the situation. A more sensible strategy would be to get to know him better, have lots of talks, and then in a few months...

She sighed, and switched on the kettle. What she needed was a hot, strong cup of tea.

Meanwhile, at the second underpass Timothy and his team were bringing the situation under control. The rain had stopped, the water was receding. It was 1:00am when he arrived home. He was shivering from the cold. He stripped off his wet clothes, had a hot shower, then thankfully collapsed into bed. Words swam through his head.

Polish Arabs facing machine guns. Cinnamon recipe, a cup of baking powder. Soupçon, yes he liked that word. He'd try it out on John.

"We heard a soupçon of gunfire the other day at that robbery."

That would fix that know-it-all Irishman.

"Huh," he could hear John saying. "What crap are you talking now?"

"It's a very common word John," he'd say, "I'm surprised you don't know it."

His last image was of his darling Elizabeth, his hands feeling the curve of her spine, her face smiling up at him.

He slept.

Chapter Three

A Misunderstanding

After a strenuous morning of training, Timothy, John and two recruits were taking a coffee break in the Bagel Shop. Timothy was about to take a bite of his hot dog when he saw her coming in the door. He drew in his breath. She was wearing the same white skirt with a fitted black top, and, he noted, high heeled sandals. Her ankle must be healed. The shop was packed. She joined the line then caught sight of him. She looked uncomfortable and turned her head away.

The first recruit exclaimed, "Wow Lieutenant, look at that, what a beautiful woman, she must be a model."

John said excitedly, "It's Mrs. Murray, Timothy. There's Mrs. Murray."

"I saw her, John, no need to shout."

With the packet of bagels in one hand and an orange juice container in the other she edged her way through the crowd.

"Mrs. Murray," John called, "there's an empty seat here, join us."

She came up to the table.

"Thank you Lieutenant, but I don't want to interrupt your meeting."

"Our meeting's over, come and sit down. Timothy, help Mrs. Murray, what's wrong with you?"

Timothy stood up, took her bag and the orange juice and pulled out a chair for her.

She thanked him but avoided looking at him. Why did she look so ill at ease?

"Well," said John, "this is nice. Boys, this is Mrs. Murray, she's from South Africa."

"How long have you lived here?" the first recruit asked.

"Quite a while now."

"So your husband's also a South African?"

"I'm a widow," she said quietly, "my husband died several years ago."

Under her lowered lids two tears trembled. One plopped onto the table, another dropped into her orange juice.

"Now look what you've done," said John fiercely, "don't ask such tactless questions."

Elizabeth leaned across and patted the abashed recruit's hand.

"But that is a normal question to ask. Yes he is; I mean he was a South African of Scottish descent. My son and I are so grateful he brought us here where we're so happy. We love the U.S. and especially Hamilton City."

"So you won't go back to South Africa?"

"No because most of my family will be emigrating soon to the U.K. My parents came to live in South Africa a few years after the war. My father died a few years ago, so my mother wants to move back there to be with her family. Also I wouldn't go back to live in South Africa, because my husband studied and worked so hard to bring us here where there are more opportunities. It would be disloyal to his memory."

There was a silence while this information was being digested, though she sensed the question about his death was about to be asked.

She forestalled this by saying, "He was a surgeon. He was lancing an infected boil, the scalpel slipped and sliced through his glove and into his hand. It was the worst possible infection. His hand and arm swelled. He died a few days later."

Timothy listened intently to this history. So much tragedy and disruption she had endured, yet she seemed to have overcome them with her good humor and sweet disposition intact. Oh Elizabeth, my arms ache to hold you, comfort you, and cherish you, he thought.

As if sensing these thoughts, she looked at him directly for the first time and smiled. Those beguiling dimples appeared.

"So you're a housewife?" John asked.

He too was moved by the sadness of her story.

She laughed, "Among other things. I also design gardens, and I'm on the board of the Hamilton City Botanic Gardens. I'm usually there several times a week to conduct tours for garden clubs, and also to give talks and answer questions. I love my work there. All my cares and sorrows seem to fall away when I'm surrounded by the beauty and serenity that has been created by all the dedicated volunteers over the years. You should visit sometime," she dimpled at John, "I'll give you a tour."

She stood up.

"And now I've probably bored you for long enough, I must go."

"Oh don't go, Mrs. Murray. We weren't bored, we loved listening to you."

She shook hands with the recruits, "It was lovely meeting you and good luck in what I think will be your successful careers."

John pushed his chair back.

"Let me see you to your car."

He took the packet of bagels from her and ushered her out the door.

Timothy watched them as they walked to her car. That son-of-a-bitch Irishman actually had his arm around her waist. What was he saying to her? She was laughing and shaking her head.

"Whew," John came back in looking flustered. "I think I could fall in love."

"Why didn't you ask her to have coffee with you?" the first recruit asked.

"I did, and do you know what she said?"

"No, what?"

"She said she'd love to have coffee with me, but she wanted to know would my wife be accompanying me. Shit, as if I'd want that nag to come anywhere with me."

"So then?"

"I said, 'you wouldn't like her, nobody likes her,' so she said, 'that's your opinion Lieutenant, I'm sure I'd like her. If she's married to a charming man like you, she must be nice.'"

Timothy was relieved. He thought, oh Elizabeth, what a darling you are. Never wanting to hurt anyone's feelings, always a kind word to soften your "no."

He called her two hours later.

"Elizabeth, are you annoyed with me? You looked so uncomfortable. You wouldn't even look at me."

"Timothy, I did feel so uneasy when I saw the four of you. I wondered if you'd told them about the other day when you..."

He was shocked.

"Elizabeth, how can you think I'd talk about you," he paused, trying to find the right words to convince her. "I respect you more than anyone I know or will ever know. I can't bear to think you wouldn't believe me."

"Well," she said, "I know how men talk, how they boast to their friends."

"Good God, I would never mention anything. In any case how many men have you been involved with? You seem so sure."

"Well, um, er, none actually, except my husband."

"And in the last few years?" he waited anxiously for her reply.

"None at all."

"So then where do you get this nonsense about me boasting to my friends?"

"Well, I read a lot and in this novel I'm reading at the moment, it's about..."

He had a feeling she was about to launch into a long description of the novel, so he interrupted her.

"My darling Elizabeth, I'm crazy about you. So you're not annoyed with me?"

"No Timothy, and I'm looking forward to our lunch. Call me next week."

"I'd like to talk some more but I've just had an urgent emergency call."

When she put down the phone she wondered what emergency he was going to and what he'd find when he got there. Lately she'd been reading the police reports in the newspaper, most of which made her shiver with fright. Armed robberies, officers being shot at, horrific pile-ups on the highway. What if Timothy... these thoughts were unbearable.

Meanwhile, Timothy was responding to the urgent emergency call, "Officer down, officer down." He noted the address, switched on his lights and siren, and in ten minutes arrived at the scene. Armed robbers in a convenience store. The clerk had been wounded. Paramedics were already arriving. Oh God, which officer had been wounded? Four cruisers, their red and blue lights flashing, were in position; two blocking the alley down which two of the robbers had run, and the other two were positioned in the street. The officers had their guns drawn. He ran to his team.

"Spread out more, call for backup, use the bull horn to warn residents to stay indoors."

He called to John, "Who is it?"

"It's Juan. He's badly wounded."

Christ, the teenager he'd recruited from one of the gangs. He had a promising career ahead of him. Shit, what bad luck.

Juan, on a stretcher, was being loaded into the ambulance.

Timothy bent down, took his hand and said, "Juan, you're going to be okay, hang in there buddy."

Juan pressed Timothy's hand, "Captain, my family..."

"Don't worry, we'll take care of them."

Four more cruisers arrived, the area was secured, and within an hour the gunmen were apprehended. With Timothy in the lead, he and John accompanied the paramedics to the hospital. Thank God for those guys, he thought, what would the city do without them? He stayed with the unconscious Juan until he was wheeled into surgery. Juan's mother and his two brothers and sister were being comforted by John.

Timothy put his arm around Juan's mother.

"Your son is very brave, Mrs. Sanchez, he's tough, he's going to pull through."

But he was worried about this family that lived in a crime-ridden neighborhood.

Without Juan's vigilance and guidance they might be recruited into one of the gangs. If only they could be moved into a safer area.

Chapter Four

An Unexpected Meeting

On Friday when he'd finished his shift, Timothy went to the hospital to check on Juan's condition. The doctor was reassuring. Juan, though still in pain, would recover. In a few months, he would be able to resume his duties. He was sleeping now. He shouldn't be disturbed.

He went home, had a shower, and changed into jeans and a T-shirt. He longed to see Elizabeth again, but because it was Friday she would be picking up her son from boarding school.

"I never make plans for the weekend," she'd told him, "my weekends are for my son."

"But why is he at boarding school? How old is he?"

"He's nearly eleven. It's a long story, I'll tell you sometime. Anyway, we have dinner together, then we watch a video. Saturday I make a big breakfast; bacon, sausages and eggs, then we go to the club to play tennis. We have lunch there and later we go to an early movie. Sunday we go out for brunch, then I take him back to school."

Timothy felt at a loose end. It was still too early to think of meeting some of the guys for a hamburger. On an impulse he decided to visit the Botanic Gardens. He was curious to see this place where Elizabeth spent so much of her time. He paid the admission fee then strolled around, amazed at the size of the grounds, the beautiful landscaping, the winding brick paths, the enormous beds not yet fully in bloom. In front of every bed there was a brass plaque with the name of the designer. One bed was fully in bloom; yellow flowers that seemed to glow. He bent down and read: "Bed of Mixed Daffodils, designed by Sylvia Smith."

He was in awe at the work and dedication that went into creating these gardens. And to think he'd never realized that this beauty existed in the city. He stopped when he saw a plaque in front of a large bed: "Designed by Elizabeth Murray." How talented she was. Oh Elizabeth, this is your world.

Then he saw her coming from the parking lot with two young boys in tow. A man came up to her and as usual she was doing the talking. Laughing and gesturing, she looked over her shoulder and saw him. Startled at first, she recovered her poise, waved at him, then walked over to him.

"Timothy, what a lovely surprise. Boys," she called to them, "meet Captain Bennet. Timothy, this is my son Alan."

They shook hands, Alan clearly impressed with the look of this tall handsome man smiling at him.

"Thank you, sir, for helping my mom the other day. She told me she didn't know what she would have done without your help."

"It was my pleasure," Timothy said, "all in a day's work."

He and Elizabeth smiled at each other.

"And this is Bruce Ward, the son of my best friend. He and Alan are at school together in the sixth grade. Bruce is spending the weekend with us."

The boys looked at him admiringly.

"Have you caught many armed robbers?" Bruce asked.

Timothy laughed.

"A few, now and then."

"Okay boys, I see Ted has my trolley. Why don't you help him load those flats into the car," said Elizabeth.

"Goodbye sir," Alan said, "it was a pleasure meeting you. I hope I'll see you again."

"I'm so excited," she said, "I'm going to plant all those annuals tomorrow."

She looked up at him.

"Do you have plans for this evening?"

"I thought I'd meet some of the guys for a hamburger."

She hesitated.

"Why don't you come home with us and have dinner?"

"Who, me?"

She chuckled.

"I don't see anyone standing next to you, so it must be you I'm inviting. Do say yes."

"Well I don't like to barge in on your family time."

"Not at all. We'd love to have you. I'm making a simple meal of steak and chips, I'm sure you'll enjoy it more than those awful hamburgers."

She dimpled up at him, "They're made from shredded cardboard, plastic and you know they're sprayed with chemicals to make them smell like meat."

He burst out laughing.

"Oh Elizabeth, the way you describe things."

He was starting to relax.

"I'd love to have dinner with you," he said.

"Good," she said, "we'll meet you at the house."

When they arrived home, the boys unloaded the flats onto the driveway, and Elizabeth opened the front door for Timothy.

"Come in," she said, taking his arm and leading him into the kitchen, "will you have a beer? You're not on duty now."

"I'd love a beer."

She took one out of the fridge and a tankard from the cupboard.

"Help yourself. I'll make a few appetizers. You should never drink without eating something." She toasted some bread and spread it with mashed avocados.

"Aren't you going to have something to drink?"

"I'll have a glass of wine with dinner. While you're sitting there doing absolutely nothing, make yourself useful and open this wine. And you can lay the table while I make the salad. Here are the placemats, the cutlery is in that drawer and the glasses are in that top cupboard."

Timothy was enjoying himself. He watched her making a large bowl of salad, lettuce, avocados, cucumbers and small tomatoes.

"I'll put the dressing on later, and now I'll peel the potatoes for the chips."

"I hope you're not using that nasty glue dressing," he teased her.

"Oh you, you like to make fun of me. Here, taste this tomato. Open your mouth."

"Wow," he said, "what a flavor. What are they?"

"Cherry tomatoes, they're coming into season now. Another one?"

"Hmm, they're really delicious. Oh Elizabeth, I love being here with you, but you haven't forgotten our lunch date next week?"

"Wild horses wouldn't keep me away. I'm looking forward to it. Come, bring your beer, I'll show you the house, not that there's much to see. It's quite small. It's the smallest house in the area. It's perfect for me. It's manageable, so I only need a maid service every fortnight. Everything's on one level. There's a good-sized family room and a large dining room. I do a lot of entertaining. And then there are just two bedrooms and bathrooms. The basement is finished so Alan has his quarters down there. I think boys like to have their own area, especially when they have friends. They can mess around, play music and generally amuse themselves."

"Elizabeth, what's a fortnight?"

She laughed.

"Two weeks, I forget sometimes that people don't understand my peculiar English. And this is the study where I love to sit and read."

"Elizabeth, so many books."

One wall was filled with bookshelves.

"Yes it was the only remodeling I did in the house. The carpenter extended and added those extra shelves."

"Have you read all these books?"

"Most of them, some, my favorites I read several times. See they're divided into sections; fiction and non-fiction. This whole shelf contains histories of the Great War and the Second World War. These are all my husband's books. He shipped them from South Africa with our furniture. He was a great reader and knowledgeable about any subject. He was much older than me, twelve years. I married him a few months after I finished high school. He taught me everything I know—the little I do know—and..." There was a catch in her voice.

"Elizabeth darling," he said gently, "you don't have to tell me. I can't bear to see you looking sad."

He took her hand and kissed the inside of her wrist.

She smiled gratefully at him.

"You're so understanding. I love talking to you. So you see here are my gardening books, and humor. I enjoy a good laugh.

This one is by an American who lives in England, Bill Bryson who wrote about his trip around America. It's called *The Lost Continent*. It's a laugh aloud book."

She took down another book.

"Look here do you remember that day I met you I mentioned Jane Austen? Well this is her most famous book, *Pride and Prejudice*. It's my favorite novel about the Bennet family. See it's your name. Elizabeth Bennet is my favorite character in literature."

"Oh Elizabeth, marry me and then you'll have the same name as your favorite character."

She beamed at him.

"Timothy darling, you're so clever. I'll give it serious thought. I'll be Elizabeth and you can be Mr. Darcy, a perfect match, only you're more handsome," she added flirtatiously.

Looking closer at the books he said, "I don't see any books about the Vietnam War. I can recommend a book that will help you understand what a tragic period we lived through. It's *A Bright Shining Lie* by Neil Sheehan."

"Yes it's important to know more about that war. I'll make a note of it. If I can't get it at Barnes I'll call the Tattered Cover in Denver. Their staff is so knowledgeable and helpful. They might recommend other books on the subject. Come, I want to show you the garden."

They went through the sliding glass doors onto a broad terrace. He drew in his breath sharply as he viewed the enormous bed that ran the entire length of the house.

"This is magnificent, surely you didn't do all this yourself?"

"No, Ted and two of his friends did the heavy work. They were happy to earn extra money on their days off. They did all the digging, the soil is so heavy and clayey. It needed loads of peat. Then they brought truckloads of compost and manure and they dug it in. The soil now is excellent as you can see, it's friable, that means it breaks up easily. I planted all the perennials interspersed with annuals. In October I'm going to plant hundreds of tulips here and in the front. Maybe you'd like to help me?"

"I'd love to and then you can teach me."

"Of course I will and when I have parties on the terrace you'll be my honored guest."

"This is a great terrace."

"The boys extended it so that there's plenty of room for the two tables. This tree is the only tree I planted, it's called 'Autumn Purple Ash' and in the fall it turns a brilliant red. It glows. When I first saw the garden I was thrilled that there were so many mature trees and shrubs, everything was overgrown of course but the boys pruned everything. They're such experts. See these shrubs? They're lilacs, but this smaller one is the Korean lilac, 'Miss Kim.'"

She led him down four wide steps on either side of which were two large stone urns.

"These will be filled with my favorite annuals."

"Was this lower level always here?"

"No. This ground sloped, which made it easier to create this separate area and the steps. Separate areas always make a garden more interesting. The English call them 'rooms.' Each area can be planted differently which makes the garden more visually exciting."

She shivered.

"It's getting chilly. Let's go inside and I'll start dinner."

An hour later dinner was ready and they all sat around the kitchen table. The boys heaved a sigh of satisfaction when they'd finished the steak and chips.

"As usual, Mom, your food was delicious. My Mom is the best cook in the whole world," Alan informed Timothy.

Timothy agreed.

"That steak was incredible," he said. "What did you do to make it so tasty?"

"Just before serving it I made a slit on the side and stuffed it with parsley and butter. But of course the steak itself is my favorite; New York strip, which I feel has more flavor than filet."

"Any dessert Mom?" Alan looked expectantly at her.

"Of course. Your favorite meringues."

She placed a plate with a meringue surrounded by strawberries and cream in front of each of them. They polished them off and were all given a second helping.

Throughout the meal Bruce had peppered Timothy with questions.

"Captain, how many armed robberies are there every week and how many bad guys have you shot and have you ever been shot?"

Elizabeth interrupted hastily.

"That's enough Bruce. Why don't you boys go down and finish your homework?"

How she hated this talk of robberies and guns. She trembled at the thought of Timothy being shot, wounded and in pain, perhaps worse even. Oh Timothy, be careful. Every time he went on his shift she tried not to think of the dangers he would be facing. The police reports she read every morning in the newspaper filled her with fear. This latest shooting of one of his recruits had given her several sleepless nights. She knew how concerned he was about the Sanchez family.

"They're so vulnerable Elizabeth, living in that gang infested neighborhood, without the protection of Juan."

"Can't they move to a safer area?"

"They don't have the money to move to a more expensive area. Of course we send patrol cars to monitor the area, but the real problem is that young fourteen-year-old girl. She could easily be persuaded to join a gang."

Elizabeth wracked her brain trying to think of something she could do to help, something that would remove that worried frown from his dear face. A few ideas had occurred to her, but it was too early to tell him. She still had to work out the details and then she would have to speak to the Board members. It was a bold plan:

1. Move the Sanchez family into the empty house on the Gardens Property.
2. The children to go to the nearby school.
3. Mrs. Sanchez to work as assistant cook in the cafeteria.
4. The daughter to help her mother on the weekends (thus keeping her out of trouble).

No, she'd say nothing until she'd ironed out all the problems. No use raising his hopes until she was certain of success.

There were a few strawberries left. She dipped one of them into the cream.

"Open your mouth, I'll just pop this in, and finish that last sip of wine. There, isn't that divine?" He kissed her fingers.

"You're divine. I can't believe I'm sitting here with you. I feel I'm the luckiest man in the world to have met you."

"Yes," she said softly, "it was Kismet."

There were a few minutes of silence while they affirmed this declaration in the only possible and blissful way.

She freed herself.

"No more Timothy, we mustn't get ahead of ourselves."

"Okay," he said glumly, no use pushing his luck too far, "so you'll be busy for the next two days?"

She nodded.

"I'll take them back to school on Sunday afternoon."

"Elizabeth, I have a few hours off on Sunday afternoon. I could give all of you a ride."

She started to protest.

"It's no trouble at all," he said.

"But you should rest before you go on your next shift."

"I wouldn't rest, I'd be thinking of you all the time and then, well, I thought afterwards I could come back here with you."

She was amused.

"Oh Timothy, you're so transparent. No darling, first of all I don't think I could resist your blandishments, and second, I've been invited to a barbecue by my next door neighbor."

Blandishments? He'd have to look that one up. But he had a feeling it meant she couldn't resist him. A couple of times he'd caught her gazing at him, her eyes soft and filled with...could it be desire? Or love?

"Okay so I'll see you Sunday and then I'll count the days till our lunch next week."

Chapter Five

An Unsatisfactory Lunch

When he got home from his shift, Timothy showered and put on a khaki T-shirt and cargo pants. He was feeling lighthearted, having spoken to Juan's doctor that morning. He had been reassured that Juan's condition was improving. This news was tempered by the fact that his leg would have to have several more surgeries. The worry about the Sanchez family was a continuous concern. Now, however, he was on his way to have lunch with the most beautiful woman in the world; a lunch without interruptions and, he hoped, not too many recipes.

When she opened the door he clasped her around the waist and exuberantly whirled her around and around.

"Timothy, stop. You're making me dizzy and you're creasing my dress."

He dropped his arms and saw she was wearing a tight fitting silky skirt with a matching top which seemed to have far too many little buttons down the front.

"But you're all dressed up. I thought you said this place was casual."

She laughed at his dismay.

"I know I'm overdressed, but it can't be helped. You see I have to give a talk at 1:30."

Shit, more talking?

"What do you mean?"

"The Botanic Gardens called me this morning and asked me to fill in for their speaker. She's got flu so I couldn't refuse. That's why I'm dressed up."

"Oh Elizabeth, I worked two extra hours on my shift just so I could have two more hours with you today."

"Darling, don't be disappointed. We'll still have the whole afternoon together."

"But what talk is this?"

"It's two garden clubs. They booked months ago, so I can't let them down. Tell you what, why don't you come with me after lunch and then afterwards we can come home and I'll make some tea and then we can really talk and get to know each other better."

"But I'm not properly dressed and besides I don't know anything about gardening."

She stroked his arm.

"You look divine, in fact you'll fit in very well. These clubs don't dress up, and of course it's about time you learned something about gardening. You're not cross with me?"

He looked down at those sparkling eyes, that dazzling smile. Who could ever be cross with her?

"I'll just put my shoes on."

He knelt down and slipped one shoe on her foot.

She giggled.

"You look like Prince Charming and I'm Cinderella."

"I'll be any prince you want as long as you're my princess."

"Oh Timothy, you're such a darling. I like you so much."

She balanced herself holding onto his shoulder.

He lifted her other foot and kissed the ankle.

"I'm kissing it better," he smiled up at her. "In fact I'll kiss it again to make sure."

He stood up and folded her in his arms, burying his face in her neck. She smelled so fresh, the light fragrance made his head swim.

"Elizabeth," he begged, "let's skip lunch, I'd much rather stay here with you."

She freed herself.

"No Timothy, we must have lunch. I'm starving, I didn't have a proper breakfast because I had to correct and add to my talk. Come, let's go!"

The restaurant was busy. They seated themselves and the waitress came up to them.

"Timothy, where did you disappear to? All the girls were like sad," said the waitress.

He looked uncomfortable. He couldn't even remember her name. Crap, was it Stacey or Tracey?

"I was transferred to this precinct, and I've been busy."

"Well we've, like, missed you, me especially."

"Uh huh," he said studying the menu and trying to avoid Elizabeth's gaze.

She stared at the girl. Quite lovely, long black hair tied back in a ponytail, slanted brown eyes and a really striking figure.

"So," Tracey/Stacey continued in a whining voice, "I'm glad I left that other restaurant to come here. Perhaps we can get together again?"

"Excuse me for interrupting your conversation," Elizabeth said, "but could we order and could you bring us coffee? I'll have mine with milk and sugar."

The waitress Stacey/Tracey shrugged and went to get their order. When she returned, she turned her back on Elizabeth and positioned herself against the table facing Timothy. Really, thought Elizabeth, any closer and she'll soon be sitting on his lap. She stood up.

"I apologize for interrupting again, but would you be so kind, if it's not too much trouble, to bring my milk and sugar?"

She moved away.

"Timothy, I'm going to look at the pastries."

She walked across to the counter and inspected the pastries—none of which appealed to her.

She was halfway back to the table when four people called out, "Elizabeth, how wonderful to see you."

Two men stood up embracing and kissing her. They offered her a seat.

Timothy peering around Stacey/Tracey couldn't believe his eyes. Shit, his lunch date was sitting at another table, one son-of-a-bitch actually holding her hand.

Pushing past the waitress, he went up to their table.

"Elizabeth, your coffee's getting cold," he said rudely.

He escorted her back to their table.

"Timothy, stop pulling me like that."

[Gentle Reader: Do not think less of our hero for what you might think of as his uncouth behavior. Remember, he had just come from a horrific shift; two armed robberies, the capture of a naked man running down the street brandishing a sword, and his worst nightmare, a sickening pile-up on the highway in which he had helped to remove a small child from the wreckage. In addition, he had worked extra hours in order to have more time to spend with his darling. It was enough to try the patience of a saint.]

"And who were those people?"

"My old neighbors, I'm very fond of them..."

"But that man was holding your hand..."

"Oh he keeps asking me to go out with him. He's recently divorced." She took a bite of her sandwich, "He's very attractive don't you think? All the women are keen on him. He's so eligible."

"Well I don't think he's attractive," Timothy said roughly, "in fact I think he's an asshole, a son-of-a…"

"Timothy, your language! I think I'll have to wash your mouth out with soap."

He apologized.

"So are you going to go out with him?"

"Oh no. I don't want to get too involved with him. I've been to several of their parties, they're charming people, but at every party he makes a beeline for me and I don't like to hurt his feelings, and besides," the dimples deepened, "I'm going out with you."

At this statement his agony receded somewhat, but then he saw with alarm that the man was coming to their table. The other three waved and called out to Elizabeth.

"See you soon, darling."

The man nodded at Timothy, then turned to Elizabeth. Timothy felt dislike well up in him. He hated the way the man had draped his sweater around his shoulders, the sleeves tied in front, the sunglasses perched on top of his head, his air of confidence and above all his carefully manicured fingernails.

Christ, what a smoothie, he'd like to get him alone in an alley.

The man said persuasively, "Elizabeth, darling, I'm having a party next week, will you come? I can pick you up and bring you home."

Crap, the son-of-a-bitch, trying to date his lunch date.

"If I'm not too busy. I'll let you know."

The man glanced at Timothy. He noted the broad chest and shoulders, the muscled arms threatening to burst out of his T-shirt. He stepped back slightly as he met Timothy's narrowed eyes. They had an ugly glint in them. This gave the waitress the opportunity to squeeze herself into the space created, making the trio into a quartet.

"Timothy," she bleated, "I have to tell you about my cousin's daughter, you know the one who was like pregnant?"

"Uh huh." He was trying to hear what the man was saying.

"...So I'd love to see you again, and we can catch up on all our news."

He bent down and kissed her (Timothy was pleased to see a bald patch on top of his head).

"So hopefully I'll see you next week."

He adjusted his sweater and sauntered off.

Timothy was outraged.

"Elizabeth, you're not going to that party, are you?"

"Oh no, of course not. And I wonder if the waitress has gone to milk a cow?"

"What cow?" He was bewildered by the change of subject.

"Oh," she said relieved, "here it comes."

"The cow?" he asked.

"No silly," she giggled. "The milk. Thank you." She smiled at the waitress.

"I thought I'd never get to drink my coffee. How long was your affair with that girl?"

What? Cow? Milk?

"Oh that waitress, well yes, as you can see she's attractive, and when she took off her..."

"That's enough, Timothy. While I do like your honesty, I really don't want to hear all the details."

"Anyway she started to get on my nerves. It's that whining voice. She kept telling me all her troubles, even sometimes when I was about to..."

"Timothy," she said hastily, "I'm warning you."

"Okay," he said. "Her mother had to have an operation to remove something or other and her uncle was having heart problems and her cat had an ingrown toenail."

She couldn't stop laughing.

"Well you get the picture. And then," he added indignantly, "she wanted to borrow money so she could study cosmetology at the Community College."

Elizabeth was impressed.

"You mean she wanted to study the universe, the stars, the moon..."

He stared at her.

"Of course not. It's make-up, you know, advising women on how to apply cosmetics. Anyhow I only gave her $100."

He looked at Elizabeth's fresh, clear skin, a touch of lipstick on that adorable mouth, a faint underlining under the remarkable eyes, "It's not anything you'd have to do."

"So how many, uh, er, intimate encounters have you had? I've met two of them, how many more?"

He looked sheepish.

"Well a few more. But they never last more than a week or two."

As they were leaving the restaurant the waitress ran up to him.

"Timothy," she shrilled, "I hope we can get together again. You were like awesome."

"Uh huh, some other time."

When she was settled in the car Elizabeth said, "Those sandwiches were delicious, were there four or five?"

What? Four sandwiches?

"Or perhaps six or seven?"

She was curious to know how many.

"Oh you mean how many women. Honestly Elizabeth, I can hardly remember their names, maybe seven or eight."

She looked at him.

"Was this in a couple of years?"

"No." He was embarrassed. "Probably a year."

"Really Timothy, you've been a busy boy."

"Elizabeth, I'm not married, and I get lonely, and besides a man has certain needs, and when women make themselves..."

"Of course, those women also have needs."

She sighed.

"And I'll tell you something else," he was warming to his theme, "the reason women make themselves available is because of Women's Lib. Their policies have been an unexpected gift to men."

"What," she was outraged, "you're talking nonsense."

"No, it's true, it's logical. Think of before the seventies and the pill women didn't just fall into bed after a few hours acquaintance. A man would court a woman, take her out to dinner and send flowers. It could take weeks or months for him to achieve his objective, and," he continued with a winning smile, "all that hard work would probably end in marriage."

"Timothy I'm surprised. You sound so cynical. I feel quite dispirited. I hope," she added, "that you don't put me in that category?"

"You, darling Elizabeth. You're in a class of your own. You're on a pedestal, my pedestal. You're like a goddess and I'd like to be your god."

"Oh you are adorable," she beamed at him and stroked his hand, "I really do like you tremendously."

Her radiant smile, those dimples made his heart thump.

She'd said he was adorable. If he was so adorable why hadn't he yet got to second base with her?

[Gentle Reader: It is becoming clear that Elizabeth has fallen hopelessly in love with Timothy. His devastating good looks, his gallantry and devotion towards her, coupled with his honesty and gentleness, filled her with an overwhelming passion. An inner voice however, cautioned her: be careful, Elizabeth, this man could break your heart.]

Chapter Six

Timothy Takes Charge

"Timothy, your car is so high. I'm finding it difficult to get in with this tight skirt. If I'm going to travel with you, you might have to get me a ladder."

"I'll get you an elevator if you like, but I rather like it when you hitch up your skirt."

She hastily pulled down her skirt.

"Really, Timothy, you're impossible."

While they were on their way, he said, "Elizabeth, I enjoyed being with you and Alan last Friday. You made me feel so welcome. I liked him so much. He's got your eyes, but I think he probably looks more like his father? He's going to be tall. He's almost your height, 5'5?"

"Yes," she said, "he looks like his father."

She turned to look out of the window.

"Darling turn on the radio, put it on that station that plays that old music. My parents loved that big band music. I'm feeling nostalgic."

He could feel her moving closer to him. Hmm, perhaps he'd put the radio on that station whenever she was in the car with him. She could sing to him and look at him with those soft eyes. He turned the sound up more, "Sing to me, my darling, I love those words."

"I'm in the mood for love."

After he'd parked, he lifted her down and was about to kiss her. She stepped back.

"No Timothy, not in public. I don't want to make a spectacle of myself. Besides we've had enough kissing and hugging."

Enough? Christ, he hadn't even started.

"Oh there's Sylvia. Sylvia," she called to an attractive girl who was about to go into the reception area. She was wearing tight fitting jeans and boots.

"Elizabeth, how lovely to see you. I'm so pleased you're giving the speech. That other woman is a real pain, she goes on and on, she's really boring," said Sylvia.

She surveyed Elizabeth.

"Wow, you look divine. I love that dress with all those little buttons, are they mother-of-pearl?"

Timothy contemplated those little buttons. He had a sinking feeling he was going to have difficulty with those later on.

"Sylvia, this is Captain Timothy Bennet. He's with law enforcement, and he's quite keen on gardening. Do me a favor and look after him while I'm speaking."

Sylvia looked at him. Would she look after him? She wouldn't mind taking him home with her. She gulped. Where had Elizabeth found this gorgeous man?

"Come with me," she took his arm, fluttering her eyelashes at him, "I promise I'll lead you astray."

Timothy was confused. Astray? If he hadn't met Elizabeth, he would have been happy to be led astray by this pretty girl.

"Oh Sylvia you are hilarious," Elizabeth giggled. "Don't lead him too far astray, I'd hate to chase after him especially in this tight skirt and high heels."

Holding onto his arm, Sylvia chatted to him as she led him into the reception area. He hardly listened to her. He was so busy watching Elizabeth as four men in suits surrounded her. One man bowed then kissed her hand. Shit, what an oily looking bastard. Another man in a grey suit put his arm around her waist and kissed her cheek. She smiled up at him and lightly touched his cheek. Timothy was incensed. His lunch date was being pawed and kissed by every man she met.

Sylvia, though very pretty, was unable to hold his attention. He couldn't take his eyes off Elizabeth as the man in the grey suit led her to the podium. He couldn't understand what she was saying, though he recognized "petunias" several times.

The speech must have gone down well, because every few minutes the members of the garden clubs laughed. When she said in conclusion, he heaved a sigh of relief, but no, she was off again, "Sir David wants to say a few words about the benefit gala which is to be held at the Gardens next month." Timothy was fuming; would this torture never end? What was that man in the grey suit saying?

"Glamorous night under the stars…$100 a ticket…Casually elegant."

What the hell was that?

Thankfully he saw that all the talking was coming to an end, but oh crap, those men were converging on her again, leading her to…what the…another room where wine, coffee and appetizers were being served. He followed the crowd into the room where he said goodbye to Sylvia. He felt desperate as he saw the man in the grey suit, his arm around Elizabeth, whispering in her ear. Her smile as she looked at him was radiant. Christ, who was he?

Now the garden club members were surrounding her, plying her with questions. Talking, talking, would she ever stop? He couldn't get near her. The precious hours alone with her were slipping away, while these idiots babbled on about petunias.

He managed to catch her eye. He jerked his head, "Let's go."

She kissed the man in the grey suit, then that foreign looking swine was again bowing and kissing her hand. All this kissing and hugging was working on his nerves.

"Come on Elizabeth," he said brusquely.

"Timothy, stop pulling me, I can't keep up with you, what's the rush?"

Before he helped her into the car he said, "Who was that oily looking foreigner who was kissing your hand?"

"Oh he's not oily. He's Italian. It's a part of Italian culture. So gallant, don't you agree?"

"No I don't agree," he said tersely. "In fact to hell with him and his culture, and who's that guy in the grey suit?"

"That's David, he's such a darling. I don't know what I'd do without him. He advises me and looks after me."

"Yes but who is he?"

"He was my husband's best friend. He's from the U.K. He flies into Hamilton City every few months. He has business interests here. Also," she hesitated glancing up at him, "he wants to marry me."

"What?" Timothy almost lost his breath, "Elizabeth, I'm begging you, don't marry him. I don't know what I'd do. Please I can't lose you now."

He could feel his chances dimming. What hope did he have against this rich man in his grey suit?

She touched his cheek, "I'm not thinking of marrying him. In fact, I don't want to marry anyone. I'm so happy as I am."

Slightly mollified, he started the car. The traffic was heavy.

"Look at that," he almost shouted in disgust, "did you see that old fart in that stupid hat? He's pushed into our lane, and not even a signal. Christ, now he's got the green light and we're stuck at the red."

"Really, your language. I'll definitely have to wash your mouth out with soap."

But she was doubled up with laughter.

"You're so ridiculous. We've got the whole afternoon ahead of us. I'm going to make you a nice cup of tea, and then I'll make you an early supper before you go on your shift. I don't want you to get hungry later in the evening, and then you'll order one of those awful hamburgers that are made of..."

"Yes, yes," he said impatiently, "they're made from shredded newspaper."

"No Timothy, I told you they're made from shredded cardboard."

Cardboard, plastic, who cared? All he wanted to do was get her home as quickly as possible so that he could...

"And," she said, "you're still going too fast, calm yourself! You're making me nervous!"

Nervous? He was nervous thinking of that man in the grey suit and his marriage proposals. There was no time to lose. He glanced down at those small buttons on her dress. They definitely were going to be a problem.

When they stopped in the driveway, she said, "Timothy I'll open the garage door. You can come in the side door, and I'll put the kettle on for tea."

When he came into the house he could hear her humming and the tinkle of china.

"Timothy I..." she stopped at the door of the kitchen, surprised. "Why have you taken off your shirt? Do you want me to put it in the washing machine?"

He didn't reply. He was removing his shoes and socks.

"No," he said firmly, "I don't want my laundry done, I don't want tea, and we've had quite enough talking. Come here."

He clasped her in his arms.

"Now look here, Timothy," she was alarmed. "We're not ready for this. We must get to know each other better then..."

"Darling Elizabeth, we're more than ready."

He was fumbling with those damn buttons.

"Elizabeth why is this dress so complicated? I can't find the buttonholes."

His worst fears were confirmed. Fucking buttons.

She was laughing at his frustration, leaning against him as he struggled with them.

"Oh Lord this is so funny." She whispered in his ear. "Those buttons are for decoration, there's a zipper at the back of the dress."

With a soft rustle it fell to the floor.

He crooned into her ear.

"I'm in the mood for love, darling Elizabeth, my treasure. Today we're going to enter paradise."

And they did.

[Gentle Reader: I'm convinced you are not a voyeur. You are not like those people who make a career out of poking their noses into other people's affairs. You would become weary of a catalog of murmured endearments and rapturous sighs and fevered embraces. You are more eager to know what food Elizabeth is going to serve Timothy. So let us go into the kitchen where several hours later he is...]

...admiring the charmingly set table, the same placemats, the crisply folded linen napkins, and a small glass bowl with blue flowers arranged in it. He felt so contented, cosseted as he watched his treasure bustling about preparing his food. He was feeling pleased with himself. He had, he felt, acquitted himself magnificently. Yes, she was his teacher, but in the activities so recently enjoyed, he had been the master. He was confident that even if a dozen rich guys in grey suits approached her with marriage proposals they would be refused.

He eyed her tightly belted robe. He wouldn't mind lifting it and...

"Timothy I don't like your bare feet on the cold floor tiles. Lift them. I'll put this small carpet under them, there, that's better, now you won't catch cold."

"Elizabeth, I stood in the rain and cold for several hours last week and I didn't get sick."

"Yes, but you've just had a hot shower, and you see it's the temperature difference. I was reading an article..."

He could sense a long medical explanation coming, so to stave it off he said hurriedly, "These flowers have the same smell as your perfume."

"It's lavender, English lavender," she was stirring the soup, "I've planted six of them in my beds. I use the toilet water made from the oils. It's light, because I don't like heavy perfumes. Smell your hands. That same fragrance is in the soap you used in the shower."

She placed the bowl of soup in front of him.

"And I read somewhere that the Queen also is partial to lavender."

"What queen?"

"Really darling," she said patiently, "there's only one monarch of any importance in the world today: the Queen of England, Queen Elizabeth."

"Oh that queen," he said mischievously. "Actually, I read in a magazine that her husband, Prince Phillip, is very popular because when he's irritated he uses the word 'bloody' a lot."

"Yes he's quite a character. Do you like that mushroom soup?" she asked anxiously. "It's Alan's favorite. I make it from scratch, using the freshest ingredients."

"It's delicious. The best soup I've ever tasted."

"Here are some toasted sandwiches. I spread the bread with lots of butter, a double layer of ham, a little bit of mustard..."

"A soupçon," he said.

"Yes but you mustn't overuse that word, try smidgen."

"Smidgen? I think I prefer soupçon. It's more French."

"Okay, then a layer of strong cheddar cheese. Then pop it into the waffle machine for five minutes."

He took the last sandwich.

"You know, I don't think you've had enough to eat. I'll make you an omelet. You must keep up your strength."

"What's wrong with my strength?"

"Well, it's just that you were quite active this afternoon."

"Darling Elizabeth, you were also quite active."

"Don't be impertinent," but she was smiling.

He stood up and put his arms around her waist.

"No Timothy, stop fiddling with me, I could burn myself."

She beat the eggs, poured them into the pan, then several minutes later slid the omelet onto a plate.

"What are these green bits?"

"Parsley, you should always keep parsley in your fridge."

"Okay, I will, and this is a wonderful omelet. I've never tasted one so delicious."

"That's because in those awful cafes the omelets look and taste like an old bathmat."

He burst out laughing.

"Oh Elizabeth, what a funny way you have of describing things."

"Next time you come I'll make you a proper meal; roast beef or that steak you enjoyed the other night and divine roast potatoes."

"And now we'll have a cup of tea, I hope you'll get used to it. It's Earl Grey. The Earl brought it back from China. It's a combination of two teas that are scented with oil of bergamot, an Italian citrus fruit. The Queen also likes it."

"How do you know?"

"Look at that box. Read that."

He read, "Twinings of London, Earl Grey Tea, BY APPOINTMENT TO HER MAJESTY THE QUEEN."

"Interesting. I wonder if that's the tea the colonists emptied into the harbor when they had the Boston Tea Party?"

She laughed.

"I hope not, that's an expensive tea to waste."

"Well," he said sipping it, "if it's good enough for the queen, then it's good enough for me."

"Now I'm going to clean up, you can help me stack the dishwasher. Always clean up at night Timothy, it's so sordid coming into the kitchen in the morning and looking at all those dirty dishes. Don't you agree?"

"I do."

He hid a smile thinking of the kitchen sink at his house filled with unwashed, chipped plates and mugs.

"And," she continued, "always sit down when you eat, it aids the digestion. I've heard of people who open the freezer, and with the door open actually eat ice cream straight out of the carton. It's so uncivilized."

He tried to keep a straight face.

"I don't believe you, that's shocking."

But that's what he did several times a week when he got home from his shift.

"Oh Elizabeth, you're so innocent and adorable."

He gathered her into his arms and thought, I hope you never have to see really uncivilized behavior, that I see every shift. Battered women and children, bloodied corpses lying in the street, it's why we in law enforcement are trained to protect people like you from all the ugliness of that terrible world. Watching her he felt contented. He'd been loved, spoiled, and served wonderful food by this darling creature who was so anxious for his comfort.

"Sit on my lap," he coaxed her.

"I don't think that's a good idea," she hesitated. "That might lead to um, you know, there's no time."

"Well I think it's a wonderful idea, and there's plenty of time. It won't take long for me to get home and change into my uniform."

An idea struck him.

"I tell you what, why don't you put on that C.D. of that old music you love, I feel like dancing with you."

He clasped her in his arms and as they swayed to the music she murmured.

"Oh Timothy, isn't this romantic? The melodies, the words of those old songs have such meaning."

He was in heaven, caressing her silken skin, listening to her sing to him, breathing in the fragrance of her perfume—the scent of lavender. Ah, but this was magic.

"Elizabeth, come with me." Gently he guided her.

"But there's no time, you'll be late."

"There's plenty of time—come."

So she went.

Later, he backed his SUV out of the garage, then sat for several minutes contemplating the amazing afternoon he'd just spent with her. Wave upon wave of happiness engulfed him.

He thought, I'll never be this happy again. I'll remember this day for the rest of my life. There must be a God, who else could have created a body so perfect; from her delicate feet, her exquisitely shaped limbs and torso, and that face—he breathed deeply—a face to make the angels sing. He shook his head in disbelief. Had he really possessed all that loveliness?

He took out his tapes of country music; Patsy Cline, Hank Williams and Chrystal Gayle. He loved them all. He hummed along with Hank all the way home.

When he came to Daniel's house he suddenly remembered—Daniel—if it hadn't been for Daniel calling him that day none of this miracle of meeting Elizabeth would have been possible. Yes, he knew the meaning of that word now. Kismet. He must do something for Daniel. He pondered, then had an idea. He'd call those great guys at the fire station, ask them to bring their shiny red truck here and take Daniel and his friends for a ride around the neighborhood. He could picture their excitement, the siren wailing, the lights flashing, the deep *parp parp* of the horn. Yes, he'd call them in the morning.

On his way to his shift he slowed down as he passed Elizabeth's house. Only the bedroom lights were on.

"Oh Elizabeth, I'll never love anyone the way I love you."

Chapter Seven

The Garden of Eden

One month later.

"Timothy, I'm home. Where are you? Oh there you are. You're still reading?"

He was sitting on the couch in the study. He was wearing shorts, a T-shirt and his bare feet were on an ottoman.

"Elizabeth, I'm so engrossed in this history of the Great War; the horror of the trenches, the tens of millions of lives lost. In the battle of the Somme alone, Britain lost three hundred thousand men. A whole generation of the brightest and the best wiped out. And all because of the assassination of that one man, the Archduke of Austria. The punitive damages Germany had to pay led to inflation and the rise of Hitler, which of course led to the Second World War and the aftermath, the Cold War, and the mess the world's in today."

"You sound just like my husband, Hugh. He often told me exactly what you've concluded. I think," she mused, "you're becoming more knowledgeable than me. Not that I know so much but you and Hugh have the same keen intellect. You both have analytical minds."

"Elizabeth, will you make a list of the books I should read next? Anything more on the Great War."

"There's a movie *Oh What a Lovely War.* It's satire, and depicts how the war was the fault of the politicians and inept military advisors. It's an eye opener."

"Let's watch it tonight. And you haven't said hello to me yet."

She sat down next to him and said hello for ten silent minutes.

She straightened up.

"That was an interesting and delicious hello. I hope you don't say hello like that to anyone else."

He said, "Don't tease me, why don't we go and…"

"No Timothy," she said firmly, buttoning up her blouse, "I want to plant those dianthus. And then I want to start dinner. I've got news for you."

"Good or bad?"

"I'll always try to give you good news. I'll tell you while we're eating."

She stood up and went to the sliding glass doors.

"Can I help you plant? I'll get my gardening boots," he said.

Hand in hand they viewed the enormous border.

"In a few months this will be spectacular. Just in time for my first party. The roses will be blooming, and the clematis too, even though they'll take another year or two to reach their full height, and of course my favorites, the fragrant lavender. Oh darling it's so exciting. How we're going to enjoy the summer."

He marveled at her enthusiasm, the sheer joy in living that seemed to radiate from her.

"Elizabeth, I think you've planted the rudbeckia in the wrong place."

"Why, they look fine to me."

"But you've planted them behind the helianthus. I read in your notes that they get tall and bushy, while the rudbeckia are shorter. They'll be hidden."

She stepped back a few paces.

"You're right. I don't know how I could have missed that. Good job you spotted that," she said.

"I'll replant all of them. How many are there? About thirty?"

He picked up the spade and started digging them up.

"And by the way, it would be more effective if you planted the dianthus in clumps of four or more instead of all in a straight row. When they stop blooming, there'll be a blank space in the front. Why don't you plant those white petunias in between the dianthus. The white stands out so well at dusk."

She hugged him.

"Timothy, you remembered what I said. You know, you've become so knowledgeable, and you've got a wonderful eye for design. I predict you'll be a great gardener in a year or two."

While she planted the dianthus and the petunias, he dug out, lifted and replanted the perennials.

"Whew," he said wiping his face on his shirt, "this is hot work."

He took off his shirt and resumed digging.

She gazed at that body she loved, and sweat or no sweat she felt like melting into his arms. There must be a God, she thought, who else could have created such a perfect specimen of maleness, the muscled calves and thighs, the powerful arms and shoulders and that face—she smiled—a face to launch a thousand ships.

"Timothy, I hope you don't wear that abbreviated garb when you work in the front garden."

"Of course not, but why?"

She said mischievously, "Because a beautiful woman in a convertible might pass and kidnap you."

He laughed.

"I'll fight her off and you can come out with your frying pan and knock her over the head and rescue me. But tell me," he said playfully, "what color was the convertible?"

"Oh you," she stroked his face, "you've done a wonderful job. Come down these steps and look at this bed. I haven't decided what to plant here. See it's a good size. Why don't you design and plant it? You've got good ideas."

"Oh Elizabeth, I'd love to try my hand at it."

He took the big fork and scooped up some soil.

"And the soil's good, look how friable it is. When can I start?"

"As soon as possible. You can start on your next day off."

"And darling, I'll go to the nursery and choose the plants as soon as I've worked out a plan. And I'm paying for everything."

"Timothy, you don't have to do that," she protested, "I don't want you to spend your money."

"Elizabeth, I've got the money. I don't want you to think I'm poor, I'm not."

"I'm pleased to hear that, and when did you acquire all these riches? Did you find a Rembrandt in your attic?"

"No it wasn't even a Picasso. When my mother died ten years ago, my sister went through a box of her papers and discovered shares in a silver mine that my father had invested in when he was young. She took the shares to the bank and discovered that the mine was still operating and doing well. When she sold the shares I got half: one hundred thousand dollars. That's how I was able to buy my house, and still have savings in the bank."

"What a fantastic story. But you might regret telling me that, perhaps I will marry you for your money."

"Elizabeth, don't tease me. Marry me, my darling. I'll keep pestering you until you say yes."

"Sweet Timothy, we've been over this so many times, why can't we enjoy our happiness? I've never known such bliss as you've given me. And look, we're living in the Garden of Eden surrounded by all this beauty."

"Yes, all it needs is an Adam and Eve. And here we are, only with too many clothes on. There's a dry patch of lawn behind those lilac bushes. Nobody can see, only that squirrel in the tree."

"But the Bible doesn't mention anything about Adam and Eve, um, you know..."

"Oh, I'm sure they must have. The Bible might have left that part out. Two healthy consenting adults, stark naked, what could have been more natural? I'm sure God wouldn't have minded. He is a wise old man."

She was easily persuaded, and for some time there was silence behind those lilac bushes. The only observer a squirrel with a twitching tail, who, it was safe to say, appeared quite surprised at the scene unfolding below him.

That night Elizabeth had made one of his favorite dinners; roast beef, new potatoes and green beans. (Never boil the beans in a lot of water Timothy, they'll turn a grayish color and taste like a wet sponge.)

"Now let me tell you my good news. I think I've found a solution for the Sanchez family."

She told him of her idea for moving the family into the empty house on the Garden's property.

"And," she said, "I've spoken to several of the Board members and they are enthusiastic, especially having Mrs. Sanchez—who is such an experienced cook—working in the cafeteria. She'll be able to earn extra money when they have events such as garden club tours and other big events. They usually have to hire outside help."

"Elizabeth, what a load off my mind. That is such great news, how can I thank you?"

"Well," she sat on his lap and put her arms around him, "I think you might have a few good ideas..."

Sometime later as they were sipping their tea, she said, "Timothy, you always ask me why I'm so fond of David, let me explain."

"Yes," he said, "I'm really curious about your attachment to him."

"You see, when Hugh died, Alan and I were like two lost souls. The shock, the fear and despair seemed insurmountable. Without David's support I never would have been able to survive it. He stayed an extra month to help me. He advised me to sell the house. It was an enormous house and garden because we'd wanted to have more children. Hugh had managed to get quite a lot of money out of South Africa and his practice was doing very well, so he wanted us to put down strong roots."

She smiled sadly, "He said, 'this will be the house we'll fill with children, the house we'll grow old in.'"

Timothy wiped away her tears. "Darling," he said, "you don't have to tell me more."

"No Timothy, I want to tell you so that you'll understand."

She continued, "David was concerned about the change in Alan's personality. He'd always been an outgoing child. He became filled with fear. He wouldn't let me out of his sight, clinging to me, and his schoolwork suffered. So when the house was sold, his real estate friend found this house. David also advised me to send Alan to a boarding school where he'd be with boys his own age, and where there are lots of sports. David said

Hugh would have hated to see his son growing up a Mommy's boy, so although it broke my heart, I agreed. And what a difference it's made. Alan as you can see is a wonderful child, full of enthusiasm again, and our weekends together are a precious time. David, who is on the board at the Gardens, managed to get me on too. So now you know why I have such a special feeling for him."

Timothy nodded.

"I do understand, but remember, my sweet, he's in love with you. Did you ever, um, you know?"

She said reproachfully, "Of course not, David would never take advantage of me in that way. In any case, I look on him as a beloved brother who protects me."

Hmm, Timothy was skeptical, but he kept quiet.

He thought, if I'd been David I wouldn't have been able to use such restraint. I'd have taken her to bed in ten seconds flat.

"No I do understand. I'm glad you told me. And by the way I was reading *Lady Chatterley's Lover*," he glanced at her slyly, "it was, how can I put it without being lewd, um, quite frank. The book was really boring, but I skipped to those er, well thumbed parts with the turned down pages, they were quite an eye-opener."

"What," she looked confused, "I can't think who would have done that. Hugh must have loaned it to a friend."

"My sweet, your cheeks have gone quite pink, even your dimples."

He was enjoying her discomfort.

"Really Timothy, you don't think I..."

"Of course not, but I was thinking..."

"Yes?"

"Well our recent session as Adam and Eve was so fabulous, maybe you can be Lady Chatterley and I'll be the gardener?"

She burst out laughing, "Oh Timothy, what will you think of next?"

But she didn't disagree.

Sometime later she said reflectively, "It's just as well you won't find the *Kama Sutra* on those shelves, you might get more bizarre ideas."

"The who? What's that you said, the suitor?"

"Forget it," she said hurriedly, "I'm sorry I mentioned it."

He held her down.

"Tell me."

She tried to twist away from him.

"I won't, I won't."

"Well I'm going to tickle you until you tell me."

"Timothy, don't tickle. I'm warning you, I'll be sick, stop that."

She was laughing uncontrollably.

"I won't stop until you tell me."

Between gusts of laughter she pointed to the top of the shelves.

"Look up there."

He loosened his grip on her and looked up. She sprang to her feet and ran into the bedroom. He chased after her and heard the key turn in the lock.

"Elizabeth, open this door. I'm ordering you as your lord and master."

"I won't. First say, 'Darling Elizabeth I won't tickle you again.'"

"Okay, I won't tickle you again."

"No, no, say, 'Darling Elizabeth.'"

Christ.

"Darling Elizabeth, I won't tickle you again."

She opened the door and laughing hysterically they fell into each other's arms.

[Gentle Reader: No doubt you have been smiling at these playful exchanges. Could any two people be more well matched? Could any couple derive more joy from each other's company? Surely this is a union made in heaven...or Eden.]

Chapter Eight

A Gift For Elizabeth

Any spare time he had between shifts, Timothy devoted to poring over gardening books. He was looking for inspiration and a design which would surprise Elizabeth when she returned in three days from San Diego.

The day before she'd left, they'd sat on the couch and paged through the books; she pointing out the gardens she admired, he marveling at the spectacular borders.

She said, "These gardens are of course out of our range. They were created by very wealthy people who had plenty of help in maintaining these labor intensive borders. Just think of how many workers there are at the Botanic Gardens, and that will give you an idea of how expensive the upkeep is for these large gardens. Ordinary people like us can never hope to achieve what you see here. So choose a bed you like, scale it down, but don't be slavish in following other people's designs. Put some of your own personality into the design."

He had narrowed his choice down to two of her favorite gardens. Hidcote Manor, the creation of Major Lawrence Johnston, an American who had settled in England and had been financed by his wealthy Winthrop mother. It had taken decades before Major Johnston's designs had been fully achieved. His garden was recognized by garden lovers everywhere as a national treasure.

The other garden, Sissinghurst with its famous white garden was created by the aristocratic Vita Sackville West and her husband Sir Harold Nicholson, on a derelict site dominated by a Tudor tower.

"We'll go to the U.K. in summer, my love, and we'll visit all these gardens. They both have hundreds of thousands of visitors every summer. How wonderful to have you with me," she said. Lying in his arms she had sighed contentedly.

"So much happiness lies ahead of us."

"Elizabeth, marry me. Then we can tour these gardens as husband and wife."

Thinking of her and the anticipation of holding her in his arms made his body tingle. How he missed her; her chatter, her singing, her unquenchable vitality and above all her laughter. Ah Elizabeth, you have bewitched me. Putting aside all thoughts of her arms, legs and all the other delectable parts of her, he sat down at the long table and drew on a sheet of paper a plan to scale, as well as a list of plants.

On the way to his shift, he marveled at the two worlds he inhabited now; the gentle new world of his beloved, the food, the books, the garden and by contrast the other world of criminals, violence and brutality.

He got home at 4:00a.m. from his shift, showered, then slept for four hours. He arrived at the nursery as it was opening. What a perfect morning, the crisp air, the bright blue sky, even the smell of the soil and the plants soothed him. The images of the savagery he had witnessed during the night faded as he viewed with a frisson of excitement the long trestle tables loaded with plants. There were few people at this hour, no crowds jostling for position in their eagerness to secure the best plants.

Pushing his cart, he made his way to the rose section. He loaded four "Iceberg" roses onto the cart. Elizabeth's favorite white rose would be the centerpiece of his bed.

A pretty girl came up to him. "Anything I can help you with?"

She was joined by another girl.

He smiled at them, causing two hearts under their denim shirts to thump.

"I'm looking for purple and blue perennials, perhaps delphiniums, campanulas and also 'Jackmanii' clematis. Do you have 'Royal Jackmanii'?"

They scurried around locating the plants he wanted.

"Also two pots of anemones." He would put one pot on the terrace table, the other on the bureau in her bedroom.

"You'll need two more trolleys, sir," said one of the girls.

Timothy made a final stop at the annual table where he selected white cosmos, "Sonata" and blue and purple petunias.

"You've got quite a planting job ahead of you," said the bolder of the two girls, "I can come and help you after I finish work here."

He declined the offer but smiled, causing another leap of her heart.

"But," he said kindly, "I appreciate your offer, some other time maybe."

As he drove off, the bold one said, "I wouldn't mind getting into that bed with him."

They both giggled.

The chief buyer and head of the perennial section came up to them.

"Come on you girls, get busy, we're going to have a rush of customers in a few hours. I was pleased to see you were helping Captain Bennet. He certainly bought enough."

"Oh is he in law enforcement?"

"Yes, he's the Sheriff in this area. But don't get any ideas about him; his companion is Elizabeth Murray, the most beautiful woman I've ever seen."

Their faces dropped in disappointment.

"Well," the bold one thought, "maybe he'll come again and bring several of his friends with him."

Carrying the containers to the back garden, he paused and looked longingly at the patch of grass in front of the lilac bushes. Perhaps tomorrow when she'd recovered from her trip, they could have a repeat performance of Adam and Eve. Even the squirrel was in its usual place, looking down at that patch of lawn and perhaps hoping for a recurrence of that fascinating scene he had recently witnessed. Timothy positioned the containers in the bed, and stood back satisfied. There was a pleasing balance between the white, blue and purple perennials. The silvery border of artemesia anchored on either side by French lavender, the elegant spires of snapdragons, and at the back on either side of the clematis, Russian sage. They would stretch the bloom period into fall.

He worked well into the early dusk, and when the last container had been planted, he stood back, convinced that his gift of love and devotion would delight her. He hurried to the door when he heard the taxi arriving.

"Oh what heaven to come home and find you here," said Elizabeth.

"Elizabeth I can't wait for you to see the new bed."

"Okay, but let me just take off my shoes."

"Is that all you're going to take off? How about a few more things?"

So as well as her shoes she took off quite a lot more...

After that, she'd admired and complimented him on the beauty of the bed. "Oh Timothy, you've done a brilliant job." They had a light supper with a glass of wine to celebrate their happiness.

She said, "Timothy, why don't you sleep over?"

"You mean sleep over the whole night? I'll wake up in the morning and you'll be next to me?"

"Yes, my darling, the whole night. So go home and get your uniform and shaving stuff and your P.J.'s."

"I don't have any P.J.'s."

"No P.J.'s? That's the best news I've heard today." She giggled.

The following morning when he came out of the shower, she said, "It should be illegal for a man to look so irresistible in the morning."

"Only in the morning?" He sat down on the bed and wrapped his arms around her.

"Timothy, this tattoo of two hands on your arm, does it have some meaning?"

"Yes, it's a symbol of our team's brotherhood. It's a bond of friendship and solidarity."

"Well, I don't usually like tattoos, but this one I definitely approve of."

He nuzzled her neck. "You smell so sweet and sleepy."

She traced around his mouth with her forefinger.

"You're doing a dangerous thing there," he said as he nibbled her fingers. "I think there's still time..."

"No Timothy, I want to start breakfast."

She scrambled away from him, but he caught her by the ankle and pulled her back.

"Don't run away from me, and there's plenty of time. I've scheduled a training session with my recruits at 9:00a.m." Her protests were feeble and easily overcome. Besides she'd had no intention of escaping him.

Chapter Nine

A Comical Encounter

Three months later.

After breakfast, as he was about to leave, Elizabeth said, "When you come back I'll meet you at your house, there are a few remodeling ideas I want to discuss with you."

"My house? What do you have in mind?" he asked.

"I thought in front of the porch a nice big bed would add character, and also white shutters on either side of the windows. They'll be perfect against the red brick."

"Surely, that'll be a waste of money?" Timothy said doubtfully.

"No darling, any money you spend will add value to the house. It's solid and well built. Your area will be valuable one day."

Later that day as they stood in front of the house, she said, "Bring me that hose, I'll show you an easy way to carve out a new bed so that you get the shape you want."

She positioned the hose so that it formed an arc.

"Get rid of all this grass, then add peat, manure and compost, then dig it all in. You'll have to water the area well because..."

"I know," he grinned, "because nothing will grow in cement. You see, I remember everything you tell me."

"I'll leave you to it then, and on your next day off, we'll go to that new small nursery on the main road. You've done such a brilliant design for your white bed, I want you to design this bed as well."

Two days later as he was pushing the cart filled with plants towards the car park, a woman ran out of the pet shop. She was dragging a dog of dubious lineage who was balanced on three legs as he strained at the leash in a desperate bid to squirt against any vertical structure in his path. A small snuffling child held her other hand. His nose needed attention.

Generously proportioned, the woman was wearing tight leggings, boots and a T-shirt two sizes too small. Though obviously dark haired, she was not one to be thwarted by nature. An enormous mop of blonde curls and ringlets was partially restrained by hairgrips and elastic bands. She let go of the child's hand.

"Timothy," she shrilled, "I thought it was you, what luck to run into you like this."

The hound, having taken a dislike to Timothy, barked to show his displeasure.

"Sharrup," said the booted one as she approached Timothy with outstretched arms.

He moved nimbly behind the cart to avoid what looked like a loving embrace.

"Uh, hi Lana."

He edged further away from her as the dog still balanced on three legs sprayed against the cart.

Another woman came out of the pet shop. She was carrying a tote bag from which a tiny dog's head peeked. She was dressed in black leather—the woman, not the dog—while horny toes protruded from Birkenstock type sandals.

"You're Timothy," she looked approvingly at him, "Lana's told me so much about you. I'm having a party on Saturday, lots of action," she snickered lasciviously. "You won't regret it." She winked at her friend.

"Uh huh," Timothy edged even further away as her dog, having also taken a dislike to him, started yapping.

The child, whose nose now needed urgent attention, tugged at his mother's shirt.

"Mom," he said.

"Don't innarupt," she shook off his hand, "I won't bring you with me no more," she added ungrammatically.

"Timothy, what fun we used to have," she patted her hair, which was threatening to collapse. "Why don't you call me sometime, I've been thinking of you so often."

Elizabeth stared. Where did Timothy find these people?

"Well Timothy," she said, trying to keep a straight face, "I'll leave you to what seems like a touching reunion. I'll wait at the car."

The mutt, having exhausted all opportunities for further splashings, squatted down. But before he could perform his other natural function, he was dragged reluctantly along by his determined owner. He left a devastating trail in his wake.

"Hey," shouted an irate shop owner, "you can't do that, come and clean this up."

But she, the child, the quadruped, the leather clad friend, and her still yapping pooch had disappeared around the corner.

Elizabeth stood with arms akimbo at the car.

"Well Timothy, I didn't realize the circus was in town."

He groaned.

"Oh Elizabeth, don't make fun of me."

"So did you have carnal knowledge of that woman?"

"I don't know if there was much knowledge, but it certainly was carnal."

He grinned cheekily at her.

"Don't be vulgar, so how long did it last?"

"Less than two weeks. Don't forget I was much younger and she was much older and with lots more experience. She showed me..."

"Stop, not another word, so what went wrong?"

"I found out everything about her was fake; all that hair, it's a wig, her eyelashes were false and..."

"Were her teeth false?"

"No those were real because when she…"

"Timothy if you say one more word I'll scream."

"And she was so boring. All she could talk about was shopping, manicures and hairstyles."

"So when was the last time you saw her?"

"Oh years ago," he thought for a bit, "she said I had such a big..."

Elizabeth swiftly put her hand over his mouth.

"Timothy, please."

He looked at her in surprise, removed her hand, kissed it and said, "All I was saying was that she said I had a big S.U.V. and would I help her move her furniture. I never saw her again."

He looked at her curiously.

"What did you think I was going to say?"

She looked mortified.

"Oh nothing."

"So I suppose you gave her money?"

"Well yes I did, you see she said she wanted to open a sandwich shop. I felt sorry for her. Only $200," he added sheepishly.

Elizabeth sighed in exasperation.

"You know Timothy, you definitely worry me. Here you are with one of the sharpest brains I've ever come across, engaged in a career that requires toughness and life and death decisions, and yet when it comes to women you're so gullible. I'm sure any woman who sets her mind to it could take advantage of you."

"No more, my darling. The only woman who could take advantage of me is you." As they drove to his house, she glanced frequently at him and thought, I adore this man, but how naive he is. I must protect him by keeping a sharp lookout for unscrupulous women.

[Gentle Reader: Will Elizabeth be able to protect Timothy from predatory females? His trusting nature makes him vulnerable to the wiles of dishonest women.]

Elizabeth went back later that afternoon to check on his progress.

"Oh Timothy, you've got such an eye for design, this is beautiful."

Her delight pleased him.

"Darling, these changes make my house look so different."

He looked adoringly at her.

"Elizabeth, let's go inside, I want to..."

"Yoo hoo," his neighbor from across the road came up to them.

Crap, always an interruption. Two more neighbors joined them.

"We wanted some advice, Mrs. Murray."

"Of course," said Elizabeth, "I'll come across and see if I can help."

Daniel, swinging a tennis racket, joined what was now becoming a crowd.

"Daniel," Elizabeth put her arm around him, "I didn't know you played tennis."

She patted his arm. "Who are you playing with?"

"No one," he replied. "My sister's doing homework and my mom is working at the hospital. I've been hitting against the garage door."

Timothy could see another neighbor hurrying towards them.

Christ, this was turning into a block party. He knew that once Elizabeth started talking it would be at least an hour before he could get her alone. Well, he comforted himself, he still had a few hours before his next shift. He'd fill those hours with all the delights she had to offer him.

"Well Daniel," she said, "you must come and meet my son Alan. He also plays tennis. Why don't you come on Saturday morning, you'll have breakfast with us and then we'll go to my club and play tennis. I'll call your Mom and ask her permission."

Daniel gazed at her with shining eyes.

"Oh Mrs. Murray, I'd love that, thank you."

"Now look here, Elizabeth," Timothy drew her aside. "There must be a limit to your kindness."

"My kindness pales in comparison to your kindness," she said.

"What do you mean?" he looked puzzled.

"Your whole career is devoted to helping people, being kind to those in dire circumstances. You, my sweet Timothy are my ideal."

[Gentle Reader: From that first Saturday and for every week for the next few years, Daniel would become a part of their circle. He and Alan would become firm friends. Daniel was to become a champion tennis player, winning many state titles. When he graduated from high school he was awarded a scholarship and with help from Timothy was enrolled at the Police Academy in Washington D.C.]

Chapter Ten

Elizabeth Plans A Gala

As Elizabeth came into the laundry room, she heard Timothy laughing in the study.

"What are you reading?" she asked. "Obviously not the Second World War or Lawrence of Arabia."

"No," he held out his hand, "come and sit with me. I needed a break from reading the heavy stuff. I wanted a laugh, and because you weren't here to make me laugh, I picked up Dave Barry's *Homes and Other Black Holes*."

He laughed at the memory, "I was in stitches right through it. Now I'm half way through Kingsley Amis's *Lucky Jim* and while I'm not quite attuned to English humor, parts of Jim's misadventures are hilarious. As you came in I was reading the episode where he drops a cigarette on the bed and burns a hole through the sheet, two blankets and an expensive Oriental rug. He gets a razor blade and trims around the holes to make the damage less conspicuous."

"I know," she said, "I've read that book several times and that passage always breaks me up."

She snuggled up to him as he put the book down.

"I'm so worried," she said.

"Oh God, what are you worried about now?"

"Timothy, do you ever get into really dangerous situations?"

He looked down at her, lifted her hair and kissed her neck.

"Where are those dimples? You must be serious. What makes you ask a question like that?"

"Well," she said slowly. "Last week I was reading..."

"Elizabeth, I've told you to stop reading those police reports in the newspaper."

"I can't help it," she said miserably, "I worry about you all the time. Last week there was a small piece about an officer, they didn't mention the name, who shot a man who stabbed his partner."

"Um, er, yes," he said, but he avoided looking at her, "that was a bad situation."

She gasped, "Timothy, was that you? You killed a man, shot him dead?"

"Yes," he said. "I did. I shot him stone dead," he said with some satisfaction, "and that's one son-of-a-bitch who won't be beating up any more women."

"Oh my God," she sat up. "What happened?"

"We'd been called to that house several times, domestic disputes, but when we got there the third time we found this woman who'd been so badly beaten," he paused. "You don't want to hear the details. While my partner was bending over her, I went to my car to give a report. As I came back into the house a man with a long knife had stabbed Bill in the shoulder and was about to stab him again. It would have been a fatal blow, so I took out my gun and shot the bastard."

"Oh my darling," she kissed his hands. "What will happen now?"

"There has to be an inquiry. Was unjustified force used, the usual, so now I'm on paid leave until the panel decides."

"How long will that take? I wondered why you haven't been on any night shifts. I thought perhaps you had vacation time."

"No I'm stuck behind a desk for the next week, and then I'll be on my normal shifts."

"But Timothy, doesn't killing someone have a psychological effect on you?"

"Sweetheart, let me explain. I was at college for three years studying criminal justice and sociology. My mother wanted me to go on and study law, but I wanted to do something practical, something that would make a difference. I suppose when we're young we're all idealists. Anyway I love my career. I've never regretted my decision."

She listened to him with rapt attention.

"Yes, initially the violence did affect me; the tense standoffs, the constant battles with the gangs, but we all handle it in different ways. Some of us become cynical, but most of us accept and cope with the various situations. For some the killing becomes a life changing experience. Those soon drop out." He sighed. "Unfortunately the only contact the public has with the police is in bad situations, they don't see our human side and the difficulties we have to face."

He continued, "You asked whether I get into dangerous situations. Of course all situations are potentially dangerous, but don't forget we have frequent intensive training exercises. These keep us alert and we learn always to have our hand near our gun. As my team came together through training we developed a rapport, that brotherhood I was telling you about, and we look out for one another. All these nutcases you read about have to be removed from the streets," he smiled tenderly at her, "so that people like you can be kept safe."

Elizabeth became more and more agitated as she listened to him. She had asked a question, now she knew the answer.

"Timothy what happens if an officer is wounded or," she gulped, "killed, what happens to the family?"

"Well, they receive a lump sum, not very much. The wife will have to work an extra job. The Police Fund doesn't have much money and of course the public doesn't want more taxes."

"Oh Timothy, I want to help."

He looked surprised. "How can you help? You mean join law enforcement, put on the uniform?" He laughed. "I must say you'd look cute in uniform, but I think you'd be more of a distraction than anything else."

"Don't be silly, of course I don't want to join. I wouldn't know which end of a gun to hold. No, I can help by raising money."

"But how?"

"Do you remember that benefit gala at the Gardens to raise money for 'Our Four-Footed Friends'? Quite a lot of money was raised, and if we had a benefit for the Police Fund I'm sure we could raise even more."

"Oh my darling, you have so much to do, I don't want you to take on more."

"But I love doing that sort of thing. It'll be easy. I promise you I'll have lots of help. Oh I can't wait to start. My notebook is on the kitchen table. I'll just go and jot down some ideas."

She tried to get up, but he pulled her back.

"No you won't. Can't you sit still for five minutes? You're always jumping around just when I'm in the mood to..."

"Oh Timothy," she murmured, as she relaxed once more against him.

That notebook remained unopened on the kitchen table for quite a while.

Chapter Eleven

Elizabeth Plans A Meeting

"Elizabeth, what a delicious smell," Timothy said as he came into the kitchen. "What are you cooking?"

"Something I haven't made for you before," she said as she turned to give him a hug.

"It's cottage pie, known in England as Shepherd's Pie. They're the same thing and so simple to make."

He put his hand on her shoulder. "Can I watch?"

"I'm making a double amount so that there'll be plenty left over for the boys tomorrow night. Ground beef, tons of chopped onions and I keep stirring until the onions are translucent. Are you hungry?"

"Starving."

"Well, make a few slices of toast. I'll put some of this mixture on top and we'll have a snack with a glass of wine. This will take about twenty minutes in the oven and when you've finished your snack would you make the dressing for this little salad of those cherry tomatoes and diced cucumbers?"

As he mixed the dressing he said, "The panel wound up the inquiry and I'll be back on my normal shifts next week."

She turned away. She didn't want him to see the dread on her face.

"I'm happy for you, my love, but I'll miss having you home at night."

She put the casserole dish on the table; the mashed potatoes covering the top of the meat were crisp and golden brown.

She dished out a large helping for him.

"There, that'll put the roses in your cheeks, good healthy food."

"Which cheeks?" he said playfully.

"Timothy don't be vulgar."

"Okay I won't be vulgar or cheeky."

They both laughed. "Elizabeth, I can't believe I'm here with you. My life was so empty before I met you, you're my dream woman. You fulfill all my needs, won't you at least just think about marrying me? I'm not nagging you," he added hastily, "but we could get engaged and that would give you time to think about it."

"Sweet Timothy, I am thinking about it. In the meantime let's enjoy ourselves."

"I can pick Alan up tomorrow and Daniel on the way back," he said.

"Darling, that would be so helpful. I'm designing a large bed for a house near the Gardens and I want to be there when the boys plant the perennials. That would save me rushing up and down."

He said gloomily, "With the house full of people for the next two days and nights I won't be able to touch you." But then he brightened. "After I drop the boys off on Sunday afternoon, we'll have the whole evening to ourselves."

"I'll be looking forward to that, too. Why don't you help yourself to some more pie? And I wanted to tell you I'm paying for coaching lessons for Daniel." As he began to protest, she said, "They're in lieu of his birthday present. It's important for him to have coaching, the coach is so impressed with his tennis. He says he shows great promise and all he needed is for his service to be straightened out, his net play sharpened up. He said that Daniel's ground strokes are superb, especially his two-handed backhand.

Alan can't even get a set off him now. I think we might have a future champion in our circle. And his mother is so thrilled. I had a letter from her thanking us for helping Daniel. She's such a good woman and she works so hard."

As they were sipping their tea, she said, "David called me this morning, he's enthusiastic about a gala to raise money for the Police Fund. He's arriving this weekend, and I want you to meet him."

"What," he nearly choked. "Are you serious? What could I possibly say to him?"

"You'll be surprised at how much you have in common with him," she said soothingly. "His background is the military; his family has served in the army for over a hundred years. He was on active duty in Cypress and Northern Ireland."

"Yes that does make him interesting, but what will I call him, Sir David?"

"Oh, he doesn't bother with his title when he's in the U.S., just call him David." She continued, "His cousin is quite high up in the London Law Enforcement, and he's looking forward to discussing your ideas for curbing gang violence. Oh my love, you'll have tons to talk about. I know you'll love him."

"No Elizabeth, I won't love him. How can I possibly love him knowing he's in love with you? Okay, I'll probably like him, and if it makes you happy of course I'll meet him."

Although he was confident of her love, at the back of his mind he still worried about her attachment to David. It went beyond their having the same background, the same interests, moving in the same circles. He envied David's ability to influence her, and her admiration of his opinions. Perhaps this was because of his support when she'd suffered the trauma of Hugh's death and the devastating aftermath of her loss. The bond between them seemed unbreakable.

"Oh Elizabeth," he had complained earlier. "As it is now, you won't let me even hold your hand in public, do you realize what agony it is for me?"

"Well," she'd said teasingly, "if you touched me I might not be able to control myself. I'd throw you down on the ground and ravish you, and wouldn't that be a spectacle and a disgrace."

Oh, how she could make him laugh. "I wouldn't mind being ravished. What exactly would you do, I want details."

But he'd watch closely when they all met on Sunday.

Chapter Twelve

David in South Africa

He was looking forward to meeting Elizabeth's sister, Mary, and her husband, Ian. He was also eager to see the house in which his darling Elizabeth had grown up.

"David, please make time to visit them. You've spoken to them so often on the phone, I'm sure you feel you already know them well. They're so grateful for your help in getting them their immigration papers. I know they'll want to thank you."

As he traveled through the Johannesburg suburbs leading to Mary's neighborhood, he marveled at the beautiful houses and gardens. South Africans, he had noted on previous visits, followed the traditional English style of gardening. Stone or brick walls screened the interiors from the outside world, allowing passersby only tantalizing glimpses through the wide iron gates. As he drew near to Mary's area he slowed down, admiring the variety of shrubs he could see through the gates. Bright red hibiscus, blue, purple and white Brunsfelsia, many azaleas and huge rose beds. The vines of dazzling bougainvillea, sweetly scented jasmine and the trumpet shaped flowers of bignonia cherere cascaded over the walls. Every house had a sidewalk garden filled with cannas, agapanthus and where it was sunny, Namaqualand daisies. Very few suburbs in the various countries he had visited had gardens like these, but then South Africans had an abiding interest and a talent for gardening, and a supply of labor needed to maintain these glorious acres. With unemployment among the blacks nearing 40%, it wasn't surprising that householders had an endless supply of cheap labor.

There were many swimming pools and tennis courts. He could hear the shouts of children splashing and playing and the ping of tennis balls. There weren't too many areas in the world where middle class and upper class people could live in such opulent surroundings. But for how much longer?

What was noticeable now was that the height of the walls had been increased, some even had rolls of barbed wire on their tops. Many had security guards at the gates. He noted sadly that South Africans were barricading themselves inside their properties. He'd read about the high crime rate, the senseless murders and the brutal rapes. The local papers were full of reports of these crimes. Those householders living in less protected areas had been ambushed in their driveways. What was even more noticeable was the absence of white people on the streets. On his previous visits, he had seen joggers, children riding their bicycles, women walking their dogs. Now all he saw were happy black people enjoying their traditional Sunday off. Music, chatter and laughter, and groups of women dressed in their blue and white uniforms making their way to their religious ceremonies. What would happen now that the majority was in power? How accommodating would they be towards the minority who decade after decade had voted for the iniquitous apartheid system devised by a delusional government?

On his first visit after the Soweto uprising, he remembered the bellicose rhetoric of the mainly Afrikaner men he had met.

"The government must send the army into those townships, clean out all the troublemakers," he had heard repeatedly.

He hadn't heard too much of that aggressive talk on this visit, just a bewilderment at the turn of events since the release of Mandela. They were reaping now what they had sowed. Unfortunately the moderate and fair minded whites would also be caught up in the retribution and upheaval which might follow.

Three million whites couldn't disappear or emigrate. The best and brightest, he thought, would do so. Jobs would disappear, but what of the poorly educated Afrikaner railway workers who had been replaced. Many of them were living in squalid camps, unable to find work; the Afrikaner language and culture would be swamped by the tide of rural blacks who were flooding into the cities.

He arrived at the address he was looking for. The guard saluted and opened the gates. Pride of India trees with their clusters of rose pink flowers lined the winding brick paved driveway which curved round to the entrance of the house which was built in the Cape Dutch style. He particularly admired this architecture. He had seen dozens of these houses on visits to the Western Cape. Unique to that area of the Cape, the style was derived from Holland, Germany and had been refined by the French Huguenots fleeing religious persecution in France. Indonesian artisans brought their skills to embellish the graceful simplicity of the central gables with their molded decorations. Most of those houses he had seen dated from the 1700's; they were reminiscent of townhouses in Amsterdam.

He stood for several minutes gazing at the symmetrical facade, the central door flanked by long narrow windows, the black shutters a pleasing contrast against the whitewashed walls. There weren't many of these houses in Jo'burg, this one was probably built in the 1930's. Before he had time to ring the doorbell, the door was opened by Mary.

"Oh David, how wonderful to meet you at last," she held out both hands. "Everyone's looking forward to meeting you."

She was a few years older than Elizabeth; pretty, he thought, but lacking her younger sister's vibrant beauty. Frown lines showed the strain she must be feeling as she faced the irrevocable decision the family had made to emigrate. The living room she led him into was gracious and beautifully proportioned. He saw many South African paintings on the walls: Adriaan Boshoff, Irma Stern, Meerkotter and several others. Elizabeth had told him her sister was an authority on South African art. Several Persian rugs were scattered on the gleaming parquet floors, and he noted lovely pieces of stinkwood furniture. What a strange twist of fate, he mused, that had taken Elizabeth from this opulence to a small house in Hamilton City where she had adjusted so well and was so happy. She led him out onto a long veranda its pillars festooned with climbing roses and bougainvillea.

Two men stood up and shook hands with him.

"Well, Sir David," said the burly man with a strong Afrikaner accent, "what do you think of the mess we've found ourselves in?"

"Oh please," said Mary. "Surely you can let the man have a drink before you bombard him with questions?"

She passed a bowl of biltong to him. He enjoyed this uniquely South African dried meat with its distinctive peppery flavor. He'd eaten it often at Elizabeth's parties. Ian, who had been overseeing the meat sizzling on the barbecue, came over, shook hands and handed him a glass of wine.

"Or perhaps you'd prefer something stronger; whiskey, brandy or a G. and T.?"

"This is perfect," David said.

And now, he thought, the inevitable questions would start.

"Would the A.N.C. be able to manage the economy?"

"What would happen to the mines?"

"What jobs would be available for their children once affirmative action in favor of blacks became reality?"

Jan Marais, the Afrikaner, moaned, "Here I've taken years of work, to build up my business, and when we leave I'll probably sell it for a song. I can't forgive de Klerk for handing over the whole bloody country to the A.N.C. in exchange for a few seats in Parliament."

"Well at least Mandela prevented a civil war," said Joan, one of the blonde wives. "The situation could've been much worse," she added.

"Yes, you and your Black Sash, marching, rallying, protesting, Free Mandela. Are you happy now that you achieved your aims?"

Jan's face was red with anger.

"It's you and your stupid government policies that have got us into this mess," she shot back. "They should have included moderate blacks in the government years ago, it could have been a gradual takeover."

Oh, oh, David could sense a serious argument brewing.

Mary intervened hastily.

"Well it's no use going over those old arguments. We've got to focus on the future. Jan and Elise are emigrating to Perth, and Doug and Joan are moving to Canada," she added.

David looked thoughtfully at them; a doctor, an engineer, and a dentist leaving the country, adding to the brain drain which had been going on for several years. A dignified black man wearing long white pants, a starched white shirt, white sneakers, and a red sash fastened diagonally across his chest addressed Mary.

"Madam, lunch she is served."

"Thank you Jeremiah. Come my friends, it's time to tuck into Ian's barbeque."

He placed a large platter of steaks, lamb chops and boerewors on the table. Salads were passed around and more wine was poured.

David enjoyed this South African custom of summer entertaining. Elizabeth was an expert at it. He helped himself to more boerewors, sausages with an unusual mixture of spices.

Jan continued his former train of thought, though he waited until Jeremiah had gone inside the house.

"Look how we built this country; the cities, the first world infrastructure, the mines..."

"Perhaps we shouldn't have built all those things," a quiet voice beside David said.

"Ag, don't take notice of my wife," Jan said impatiently, "Elise can sometimes talk nonsense."

"But that's a point of view I haven't heard before," David said, "and quite interesting."

He glanced at her sitting next to him. He hadn't taken much notice of her, she had been so quiet. Now he was struck by her loveliness; yes a fine example of Dutch beauty, the pale blue eyes, the fair hair and the flawless complexion. "We were building on other people's land. We didn't even ask their permission."

"Listen to her," said her husband contemptuously, "if we hadn't developed the country, the blacks would still be living in grass huts and fighting and killing one another in tribal wars."

"Maybe they would have been happier living as they'd always lived, without interference from outsiders," she countered stubbornly.

"God in heaven," Jan spluttered. "Listen to her, after all the sacrifices and hardships our people suffered."

"If we'd stayed in our own countries it wouldn't have been necessary to have made all those sacrifices," she insisted.

David felt a spirited family row was about to erupt. He was relieved when Mary called from the head of the table.

"Anyone for fruit salad?"

She ladled out a mixture of paw paws, guavas, mangoes and the pulp of granadillas, also known as passion fruit.

"Did you see yesterday's newspaper?" Joan asked as everyone helped themselves to ice cream, a perfect complement for the fruit salad.

"Those liberal swine," Jan exploded. "Are you still reading that tripe? I say bugger them and the rubbish they put out about the Rainbow Nation."

David could hear Elise giggling softly next to him. Joan looked offended.

"What I read is none of your damn business."

"Calm down Jan," Ian said soothingly. "Let's focus on what's important, our move."

After the guests had left, he, Mary and Ian strolled around the garden.

"Have you seen what's happened to Hillbrow?" she asked David.

"Yes," he replied. "The son of one of my director's took me two days ago and I'm still feeling depressed by what I saw; the litter everywhere, prostitutes black and white plying their trade at every corner, well dressed pimps touting for customers. What shocked me the most were the young white girls lying on the sidewalk, drunk. The buildings looked rundown, laundry hanging from the balconies, vendors had spread their wares out on the sidewalk, it was chaotic," he continued.

"Those African vendors didn't seem to resemble the local people. Who are they?" he asked.

"That's because they aren't local," said Ian. "They come from as far away as Somalia and Nigeria. A lot of Zimbabwe refugees too. Figures I've seen put the number of foreigners from Africa at over one million. If you remember, the apartheid army used to guard the borders. Mandela wanted the borders opened to allow the rest of Africa to enjoy the riches of this country and also to show his appreciation for the support those countries gave during the apartheid era. I think though," he went on gloomily, "the A.N.C. might regret that decision, because these newcomers have brought AIDS with them, and then the resentment among the local people against these foreigners who have set up businesses in the townships. Alexandra, especially, will eventually lead to trouble. The Somalians are sharp business traders, they've been very successful. No I think there'll be trouble ahead."

"So areas like Hillbrow will continue to deteriorate, one can only hope that the government will see the folly of allowing this to happen and do something to stop it. We used to love going into Hillbrow," Mary said sadly, "there were some good restaurants and an excellent book shop. There was a village-like atmosphere, lots of small shops, most of them are empty now. Although," she laughed, "I did see a witchdoctor is in business in one of them, selling potions for all sorts of ailments including AIDS. I also saw powders to stop the tokolosh from climbing onto servants beds. You've heard of the tokolosh?"

"Yes," David laughed, "Elizabeth told me so many funny stories. The one about the tokolosh, a small man who tries to climb on the servants beds. They put bricks under the legs of their beds so that he can't climb up."

"Anyway we won't be making any more trips into Hillbrow until it's cleaned up. Most of the buildings are now home to drug dealers with a good sprinkling of brothels."

"What I couldn't get over was the attitude of the young man who was driving me around," David said, "I asked him what would happen to those young girls lying in the street, and he said, 'they all have AIDS, they won't last long.' His indifference really shocked me. He said he was getting out of this hellhole of a country. He was off to Australia. I really took a dislike to him."

"Well, it's just as well the topic of Hillbrow didn't come up when Jan was here. He's so bitter, one can't blame him; watching his people being debased, the poorly educated Afrikaners unable to find jobs, the young girls prostituting themselves. It's a tragedy. I hope when he settles down in Australia he'll keep his ranting to a minimum, otherwise the Aussies will hear an earful," Mary said.

"David, what do you honestly think the future will be for our country?" they asked.

"It will take some time for the A.N.C. to settle into running this sophisticated economy. Having been in exile so long, they will have to find the people who can accomplish this, the next few years could be difficult. One problem they face is fulfilling all the promises they've made to the poor majority, but," David continued, "South Africa is a rich country and managed properly will continue to prosper. They must bring unemployment down which will lead to a lower crime rate, although a worry are the attacks on the white farmers. Let's hope they don't follow the example of Zimbabwe." He smiled at them. "People like Jan Marais will have to change their attitude if they want to be a part of this new South Africa, a nice chap," he laughed ruefully, "but a bit of a lunatic."

They continued their stroll, David admiring the expanse of immaculately maintained lawn and flower borders.

"How many staff do you have to keep all this looking like this?" David asked.

"Four permanent and several odd jobbers. You see when Dad died, we bought the house from Mom. She wanted to go back to the U.K., so we built an extra servant's room and upgraded quite a lot in the house."

She sighed. "We also made a lot of changes in the garden. That summer house you see there. Then as the crime rate increased we added two feet to the top of the walls. And no doubt you noticed the security guard and new gates which added to all the extra expenses."

The frown lines on her forehead deepened.

"Every week seems to bring more aggravation. The cost of living has gone up. I know how concerned Ian is even though his practice is successful. How foolish we were not to conserve our capital. All that money wasted now that we're leaving. Do you know, I'll be relieved to get rid of all the responsibility of this house and garden. The servants who rely on us for everything from their clothing, food and all their medical welfare. And it's not only them. It's all their relatives from their villages, who can stay up to two weeks sometimes more. It's becoming impossible to cope with all these visitors. Ian has become nervous, allowing all these strangers onto the property. I don't think I told you about a terrible murder a few blocks from here. I don't want to go into the details, but it was horrific, and it turned out it was the gardener's son and several of his friends. So Ian has put his foot down. No more visitors." She sighed deeply. "Yes it will be a wrench to leave this lovely place where Elizabeth and I grew up but," she was watching Ian as he inspected the pool, "Hugh was the clever one. After the Soweto riots he saw the writing on the wall. He was young enough to study and pass the American exams, while we were living in a fool's paradise, and now Ian feels he's too old to study. It's much easier to emigrate to the U.K. where there's reciprocity, especially as he did two years at Guy's Hospital."

As he drove back to his hotel, he reflected on everything he'd seen and heard in the last week. His directors had become alarmed at the ominous statements from certain cabinet ministers; the government takeover of the mines.

"Perhaps, David, you should go and assess the situation. It might be wise to limit our exposure there, concentrate more on Canada and the U.S."

He had assessed the situation. He had made his decision which he would present to his Board on his return to the U.K. Arriving at the hotel, he went up to his room, packed his bags, then phoned the airlines to confirm his plane's departure time.

The visit to Mary and Ian had depressed him. The fear and insecurity he had seen in their eyes had touched him, even the brash rhetoric of Jan Marais was a reflection of that fear. But they would succeed. He had no doubt of that. South African men, talented, hard-working and determined would make new lives for themselves, though their ties to their country would always be strong. They would watch from afar as events unfolded in their beloved South Africa.

He sat for another hour thinking of Elizabeth, how he adored her, desired her. Perhaps on his next visit to Hamilton City he would be more assertive, more persuasive. Surely this time he would be successful and his dream of marrying her would come true?

Chapter Thirteen

A Dream Deferred

David sat on a bench near the Gardens' entrance. He was waiting for the arrival of Elizabeth and Timothy. While he waited, he cast his mind back to the first time he'd met her. It was at an afternoon tea in Jennifer's garden. He had met Hugh the month previously when he'd had minor surgery on his arm.

"David," Hugh had said. "Meet my wife Elizabeth and our son Alan."

He had literally lost his breath at the sight of the most stunning looking young girl he had ever seen.

"Sir David," she had smiled radiantly up at him. "You're the first Sir I've ever met, but no one told me a Sir could also be good-looking."

"Oh," he said, matching her playful tone. "What about charming as well?"

"That would be a triple whammy." She had laughed as the dimples in those flawless cheeks deepened.

No artifice about her, and so much confidence he had never seen in such a young girl.

Hugh had smiled indulgently. His adoration of this perfect creature was obvious.

"Elizabeth is a knowledgeable gardener and a very good cook. When we move into our new house, we hope you'll visit us David."

He had visited them many times, and his love for her (unhappily unrequited) over the years had grown into an obsession.

She had made him laugh at her inexhaustible fund of stories of growing up in South Africa.

"Tell me again about the tokolosh, I find it fascinating."

"I've told you a million times, aren't you tired of hearing about him?"

"No," he'd said, "you tell it so well, and each time you embellish it."

"Okay, so he's a small man, a dwarf really, and the servants were all terrified of him. The women especially, because he wanted to climb onto their beds. So they put bricks under the legs of their beds to raise them up, and so of course, the beds were too high and he couldn't climb up."

At this point in the story he was doubled up with laughter; her manner was so serious.

"What did they think he wanted to do to them supposing he managed to get on the bed?"

"Well," she had said gravely, "I don't think his intentions would have been honorable. Despite his size he was extremely powerful."

How adorable she had looked as she'd recounted this story. He suspected she half-believed this nonsense.

One day strolling in the garden which Elizabeth was transforming into what would become a spectacular English garden, Hugh had said to him, "David, I've been thinking of taking out a life insurance policy—oh don't worry, there's nothing wrong with me. I'm as strong as an ox. It's to protect Elizabeth in the unlikely event that something should happen to me. She would have no means of supporting herself and Alan. As you know, I married her soon after she matriculated. Alan was born a year later, so she never went to Varsity. She has no protection. What do you think?"

He had agreed. She needed that protection. Then the unthinkable had happened; the accident during surgery, the scalpel slicing through his glove and into his finger, the virulent bacteria entering his blood stream. It had proved fatal.

On hearing the news, he had flown to Hamilton City.

"Oh David," she'd sobbed in his arms, "what will I do without Hugh, what would I have done without you?"

He had stayed an extra month, helping her, advising her. He had recommended her to the Gardens Board, where her talent in designing had been recognized.

Over the years he had had affairs, but none of them had held his interest. Even the beautiful and intelligent women he'd found boring. When he compared them to Elizabeth, they seemed pallid, devoid of her sparkling personality, that innate joy that affected everyone she came into contact with. He had waited almost two years before he'd broached the subject of marriage. Holding her in his arms, breathing in her subtle lavender perfume, he'd been disappointed at her response.

"David darling, you know I love you dearly. Can you give me more time?"

Yes she loved him, but not in the way he so desperately wanted. A few months ago, she'd told him of a walk she'd taken—the accident in an isolated area, the rescue by a police officer, and most alarming, her meetings with him for coffee and lunches. He hoped that this was just a light romance. Elizabeth, he knew, would never indulge in casual affairs. The men who flocked around her were treated with a friendly reserve. Her sweet nature offset the annoyance any of them might have felt at her spurning them.

He sighed, now she wanted him to meet this Captain Bennet ostensibly to discuss the benefit gala in aid of the Police Fund.

He saw their car, then Alan and a friend ran up to him.

"Uncle David," Alan shook hands, "this is my friend Daniel Wentworth."

A nice lad, he was the child who had also helped Elizabeth.

"Mom, we're going to look at the waterfall to see if it's finished," Alan called to her.

As she and Timothy approached he realized that this was no light romance. Though not even their hands touched, the sexual spark between them was palpable.

Timothy was the handsomest man he'd ever seen. A shade under six feet, his physique was perfectly proportioned. His profile, David noted, could have appeared on a Roman coin; his dark good looks and confident air were impressive. His face was serious, brooding almost, but when he smiled down at Elizabeth his expression softened. The intensity of his gaze disclosed to David that this was a woman he had possessed.

Elizabeth, her face glowing, had never looked happier. David thought, could he begrudge her this happiness after the tragedy she had endured?

Oh my darling, he mourned inwardly, I think I've lost you.

"Captain Bennet, this is Sir David Knightley."

"Oh please," said David, smiling and shaking hands. "We don't have to be so formal. Timothy, call me David."

"Yes," replied Timothy. "After all we're not in a Jane Austen Novel."

David burst out laughing.

"Timothy, I can see Elizabeth has had an influence on you."

They sat on the bench with Elizabeth sitting opposite them on a chair. They spoke first of military matters, the Great War and its aftermath. Elizabeth could see that David was impressed with

Timothy's knowledge, his grasp of the facts leading up to that war. The conversation turned to Law Enforcement. David was interested in Timothy's ideas for curbing gang violence.

"Timothy, my cousin at London Law Enforcement will be interested in these radical ideas of combating these problems. These will certainly give him food for thought."

Elizabeth sat quietly listening to them. She was happy to see that these two men whom she loved were getting on so well. She gazed fondly at David. How distinguished he was with his military bearing, his fair hair starting to silver at the temples, his warm brown eyes.

After half an hour she stood up. "I'll leave you to it, I'm going to talk to Ted."

Immediately, David could sense Timothy's interest waning as his eyes followed her.

After a minute of silence, David said, "Shall we join them?"

As they came up to her she said, "Oh David I'm so excited."

"Well Elizabeth, isn't that your usual state?" he replied.

"Oh don't tease me. Ted has some wonderful ideas; moving the disc jockey and all his equipment further back, then we can fit in some extra tables, and then there'll still be room for dancing, and," she went on, "Le Delice Gourmet is donating the appetizers and desserts, and the Vinery promised a case of champagne."

"Did you speak to the manager personally?" David asked.

"No, I called him."

"Well," said David, "if you go into the store I'm sure that when the manager meets you he'll donate three cases."

They had lunch in the cafeteria.

"I must say the quality of the food here has improved since Mrs. Sanchez has taken over," David said. "These tacos are delicious."

He could sense their anxiety to be alone, they wanted to leave. He felt an overwhelming sadness as he watched them walking to their car.

He thought, my dreams of happiness have been shattered. Oh Elizabeth, why did you go for a walk that day?

The gala was a great success. Afterwards, walking to the car, Elizabeth said, "Oh darling, what a wonderful evening, I'm so happy. Didn't you enjoy it?"

"No Elizabeth, I didn't enjoy it. I was in agony watching you dancing with all those men, and," he said indignantly, "you danced three times with David. What's more," he added accusingly, "I saw him whispering in your ear. What was he saying?"

"Timothy don't be ridiculous. He was singing that song to me. We both love it. It's from the Second World War. Vera Lynn used to go to the station when the troop trains were leaving, and she'd sing it as the trains pulled out. That song is seared into the memory of anyone who lived through that war. It's been passed down from one generation to another."

She sang it softly to him.

"Aren't the words evocative? David and I felt quite nostalgic listening to it."

"Well I'm not interested in that nostalgia. I didn't like seeing David holding you so closely."

"Don't be jealous. You know it's only you I love."

When they got home, Timothy said, "Oh Elizabeth, I wish I could take you to a desert island where we'd be alone with no interference or interruptions."

"Oh you'd soon get bored with me."

"Never. Bored with you? Impossible. You'd keep me amused with all your stories and jokes, maybe even some of your recipes."

"And what would you be doing?" she asked.

"I'd be practicing and refining my amatory skills on you." She put her arms around him.

"Why wait till we get to that desert island? You can start practicing right now. After all there's no time like the present, and Timothy, my sweet, practice makes perfect."

So he practiced to their mutual satisfaction for some time.

***

The reporter from the social page gushed as she described the gala.

"Glamorous Night Under the Stars. Brilliant social event to remember. Handsome officers, beautiful women, delicious food, lively music and sparkling champagne. Everyone of importance was there." Having run out of adjectives, she added, "It was a sold out event to raise money for the Police Fund."

"Pictured below are the chairpersons, Sir David Knightley, Mrs. Elizabeth Murray, Captain Timothy Bennet and flanking them, Daniel Wentworth and Alan Murray."

Daniel cut the piece out of the paper and added it to the pile of remembrances in his treasure box.

Chapter Fourteen

The Reward

As they strolled around the garden, Elizabeth said, "When I get back from San Diego we must plan a final dinner party on the terrace. It'll soon be too cold to eat outside."

"Do you have to go? Isn't there anyone else who can go?"

"No darling, David left for the U.K. yesterday and the Board wants me to be there."

"I hate these separations," he grumbled. "But I guess I'll have lots to do while you're gone. I'll have the whole day off on Tuesday so I'll work on those borders and get them into ship-shape condition."

As she walked through the concourse of the Hamilton City Airport, Elizabeth was surprised to see John hurrying towards her.

"Why John, how nice to see you, where are you off to?"

"Nowhere," he replied. "Do you have luggage to wait for?"

"No, I only have my carry-on bag."

He took her arm and guided her to two vacant chairs.

"Elizabeth, I'm sorry to give you bad news. Timothy's been wounded."

She caught her breath. "What? Oh God what happened?"

"It was a bad hostage situation, a Code 4. Gang members had tricked two of our new recruits into going into the house." He paused for breath. "Tyrone, the black teenager Timothy had recruited from a gang, had been wounded. He and the other recruit who was tied up were in the laundry room."

"What did they want?" Her face had paled, her hands were shaking.

"They wanted three of their leaders released from jail, and free passage for all of them to Mexico, plus $50,000. We'd been negotiating with them for two hours. They said they'd rigged the house with dynamite and they threatened to blow the house up if we didn't give in to their demands within an hour, or if we tried to rescue the recruits. The S.W.A.T. team had arrived as well as more reinforcements."

He put his arm around her as he continued.

"Timothy was worried about Tyrone. Perhaps he was bleeding to death. The situation was becoming desperate. Timothy told me to order everyone to the front of the house, to cause as much distraction as possible. He even called for another helicopter to fly overhead. The perimeter for several blocks was secured. The press—there were dozens of them—to stay well back. He said to have the medivac team on alert. He went around through the unlocked side garage door and with his shoulders smashed through the door into the laundry room. He carried Tyrone out, but when he went in again two gunmen, who must have sensed something, appeared. Timothy shot one of them, the other one fired at him, one bullet hitting him below the shoulder, another one grazed his head. Then they ran out. Timothy hoisted the recruit over his good shoulder and brought him out. A few minutes later the house exploded. Elizabeth, it was like a scene out of hell. Thirty cruisers and squad cars, their lights flashing, the helicopters overhead, the house engulfed in flames. Elizabeth, Timothy saved those boys from a horrible death."

She tried to keep calm.

"John, how badly is he wounded?"

"I don't know. I left as he was going into surgery. The doctors will be able to tell you. Elizabeth, before he lost consciousness he was calling for you. The doctors want you to be there when he comes around."

A cruiser driven by a sergeant drove them to the hospital. Her legs were shaking as John hurried her inside.

The surgeon and several colleagues came up to her.

"Mrs. Murray we're glad you're here and we can assure you that the surgery went well. The bullet fortunately missed the Captain's vital organs. Two ribs were smashed, but they will heal in time. His lung has collapsed, but that in time will reinflate. He's had a blood transfusion, because he lost quite a lot of blood. The bullet that grazed his head didn't do too much damage. It'll take a few weeks to heal, though it's possible he might suffer from headaches."

Sitting in a chair next to his bed in the I.C.U., she waited for the anesthetic effect to wear off. As she held his hand, he opened his eyes briefly.

"Oh God, Elizabeth, I thought I'd never see you again. Don't leave me."

A week later as he was sitting up in bed she said, "You look quite jaunty with that bandage around your head. Timothy I want you to come and stay with me, so that I can look after you."

"You mean stay all the time, for good?"

She smiled. "You can stay until you get tired of me."

"But what about my house?"

"Don't worry," she patted his hand, "I've spoken to the real estate agent and she says it'll be easy to rent, especially if it's furnished. All we need to do is pack up your clothes. My darling, you're going to rest and eat good food."

A few weeks later as he sat in the rocking chair in the bedroom, she came in with a tray with chicken soup and sandwiches.

"Oh Timothy," she exclaimed, "look at that tree, it's turned."

They gazed in wonder at the fiery mass outside the window.

"Put the tray down, come and sit on my lap."

"What about your soup? It'll get cold."

"You can always warm it up again."

She lowered herself carefully onto his lap.

"You don't have to be so careful, I won't break."

She put her arms around his neck and drawing him close, murmured in his ear.

"Oh Timothy, I love you so. I've loved you from the first moment I saw you. I will marry you."

He started, then held her away from him.

"What did you say? Look at me and say that again."

Silhouetted against the glowing tree she looked into his eyes and said, "I will marry you."

It was an image he would never forget.

A month later in the reception hall of the Law Enforcement building, Timothy, flanked by the two recruits he had rescued, was awarded the city's medal for bravery. Elizabeth, standing with Alan and Daniel, fought back tears as the medal was pinned on him.

"Captain Bennet," the Chief Commissioner announced, "has been promoted to Commander and will take up his duties in this building next week."

As the applause died down, the Chief looked at Timothy and Elizabeth and smiled.

"The other good news is that Commander Bennet and Mrs. Elizabeth Murray are engaged and will be married in the spring."

Well-wishers surrounded them. There was a happy buzz in the room.

Kalisha Taylor came up to Elizabeth and taking her hands said tearfully, "Our family will never forget how the Commander saved Tyrone's life."

Elizabeth embraced her, "And how well he's recovered. I hear there's a promotion coming his way."

"Yes, we're so proud of him. And let me introduce you to my other sons, Nelson, he's six and Mandela, he's ten."

Elizabeth laughed delightedly. "What wonderful names. I'm sure they'll live up to the honor of being named after a great man."

Jean Sedicki also came up to Elizabeth to offer her congratulations.

"I took your advice and visited Poland. Everything you told me was true. I was visiting a village where I'd contacted some relatives and there I met Stefan, and we fell in love. He's an engineer and he was installing a new water system in the village. He's got a work permit to work in the U.S. He's already been hired by the city. There he is talking to Timothy."

Elizabeth looked at the fair haired man and said, "Didn't I tell you that Polish men were good looking?"

They laughed and hugged each other.

Fairy Tale Wedding at the Gardens was the headline on the Social Page. "The Wedding of the Year took place at the Botanic Gardens. Every V.I.P. in the city was there to share in the happiness of the bridal couple, as well as relatives from the U.K. and Ohio. The bride wore a pale blue chiffon cocktail-length gown designed by Francine of New York. Long waisted and tightly fitted, it flared slightly from below the hips and was off the shoulder, which showed to perfection the pearl choker inherited from her grandmother. Her hair, falling in soft waves, was sprinkled with small blue and white flowers. Mrs. Bennet was a vision of ethereal loveliness," the reporter gushed, then continued effusively, "she carried an exquisite posy of heavenly white roses interspersed with sprigs of English lavender."

"The groom, handsome in his Commander's dress uniform chose as his honor guard the team of officers with whom he has worked for many years. The happy couple will spend their honeymoon at the Broadmoor Hotel in Colorado Springs."

"Pictured below are Commander and Mrs. Bennet standing under an arch of magnificent pink and white roses. Pictured on the left are the bride and groom flanked by Alan Murray and Daniel Wentworth."

Daniel put the cutting onto the growing pile of remembrances in his treasure box.

[Gentle Reader: This love story has at last come to a satisfactory conclusion. A beautiful couple living blissfully in their Garden of Eden. But...not so fast, wasn't there an unpleasant incident in the original Garden of Eden, involving, if you remember, a serpent....]

Chapter Fifteen

A Serpent Enters The Garden Of Eden

[Gentle Reader: As you know from the Old Testament, God created Adam and Eve and gave them the Garden of Eden in which to live. What a carefree life they led: no gas or water bills to pay, no homeowner dues, and no neatly dressed gentlemen clutching fistfuls of religious tracts banging on their gate. Into this paradise a serpent slithered...]

"Hi," he said to Eve, leering at the strategically placed fig leaf covering her, um, well, interesting parts.

"You two seem to be living on the fat of the land, and all this delicious fruit. But I notice you haven't tried any of the apples from this tree."

"God told us not to touch that tree," she replied primly.

"Oh I'm sure you misunderstood Him," he said persuasively. "Why don't you try just one?"

So she plucked an apple from the forbidden tree and took a bite out of it. Adam, who wasn't the sharpest knife in the drawer, ignored this exchange; he was eating a (Bosc) pear, the juice running down his chin.

"Oh Adam," said Eve, "take a bite of this apple, it's delicious." So he did. When God saw this he was, to put it mildly, incensed.

"Thou hast disobeyed Me, and now thou wilt suffer," He thundered (or words to that effect).

He added vengefully, "Thou wilt be banished from the Garden of Eden to maketh your way in a cruel, cold world."

And with a flash of lightning He disappeared to be seen next on Cloud Nine enjoying a nice hot cup of tea (to calm His nerves), brought to Him by an archangel who had been judging a competition among the other angels to see who had the shiniest halo.

"Oh sweet Jesus," God moaned, "just imagine the sins those people are going to commit in the New World Order. Well, I'll have to send my Beloved Son to save them, but," he added thoughtfully, "we'll have to search for a Virgin."

Satan, also known as Beelzebub, was sitting in a corner sulking (he'd lost the shiniest halo award), when he heard the ruckus from above, and God's pronouncement. He did a little tap dance on his cloven hooves.

"If I'm hearing right, there'll be plenty of work for me to do in this New World Order."

Beelzy, as he was affectionately known to his followers, called all the Satans together. When he told them of this new turn of events, they capered about gleefully.

"Okay, enough of that, settle down, and form lines in front of the sins you want to be in charge of."

He indicated placards that had been set up with the names of the various sins on them: murder, theft, Ponzi schemes, fraud and adultery/sexual crimes. The line in front of adultery/sexual crimes was triple the length of the other sins.

"Okay, you guys, calm yourselves. I'm going to see how that fire is coming along."

He found the Satan in charge of the fire dozing in front of the small blaze.

"Wake up, you lazy good-for-nothing. Stoke that fire, we'll be having lots of souls coming down here very soon, and for the next couple of million years order double loads of coal."

"You betcha," said the Satan, grateful to be doing something useful.

Satisfied that everything was under control, Beelzy called up to God.

"And good luck with your search for a Virgin. Heh, heh," he chortled.

As a result of this upheaval, our world has inherited the following: War, Pestilence, Famine, Income Tax, Telemarketers, Lobbyists, Political Ads, Hip Hop, and body piercings in odd places.

And all because of that ****ing apple.

As the gates of Eden clanged behind them, Adam and Eve saw, to their shame, that they were nearly naked. Their fig leaves (a forerunner of the thong which was to become popular millions of years later), were clearly inadequate. They scrambled around gathering leaves and small branches with which to cover themselves. No sooner had the gates shut behind them than they started arguing.

"Haven't I told you a million times not to talk to strangers?" Adam fumed.

He was interrupted in his harangue by two neatly dressed gentlemen clutching fistfuls of religious tracts.

"Get the hell out," growled Adam, "can't you see the sign, 'No Soliciting'?"

He turned once more on Eve. "How stupid you are to have listened to that serpent?"

"Don't you dare shout at me," Eve said shrilly. "Why didn't you come and listen to what that son-of-a-bitch was saying to me?"

"Tut tut, your language," Adam said sternly, "I might have to wash your mouth out with soap; that is, if I can find any soap."

"Oh to hell with you." She flounced off, clutching the leaves to her nether region.

Hmm, Adam eyed her shapely figure. He hadn't appreciated how hot a babe Eve was. Well he'd make up for lost time now. He adjusted his fig leaf and hurried after her. This was his opportunity to start a family.

Clearly what these two were going to need was a lecture on Family Planning, Marriage Counseling and Family Values.

Chapter Sixteen

Tiffany Takes Center Stage

[Gentle Reader: It was the fourth year of their marriage, and you'll be pleased to know that Timothy and Elizabeth were as much in love as when they'd first met. In fact their love had intensified and deepened to the extent that they were seldom apart. They were blissfully happy in their Garden of Eden.]

They kept to their routine of weekend morning breakfasts with Alan and Daniel, but the boys had active social lives; Daniel being absent for most weekends playing in tennis tournaments.

The Commissioner of Hamilton City retired. Timothy was promoted to this post, and his responsibilities increased as did his work load. His bold initiatives for limiting gang activity had met with success and he was becoming known nationally for his methods in decreasing the crime rate in Hamilton City.

Elizabeth had been commissioned by the Board to write a history of the Gardens from its inception with a book to be published in time for the 50th anniversary celebration.

There had been some reorganization in Timothy's office. Of the dozen employees there, four had resigned due to pregnancy and marriage, and while three of these positions had been filled, the last remaining vacancy—that of his Personal Assistant—still had to be filled.

***

When Tiffany Horseley entered the foyer of the Law Enforcement and Justice building, she attracted many appreciative glances from the men—some of them in uniform—who were hurrying to their offices. She was wearing an abbreviated skirt which displayed her magnificent legs. Her long blonde hair (some of it hair extensions) fell over one eye. Many bangles and bracelets jangled as she swept the hair back with a hand, the fingernails of which were long and painted a bright red. Tall and athletically built, her height was increased by her three inch stiletto heels.

She strode confidently across the foyer. She was impressed by what she saw. Granite flooring, paneled walls and a huge central dome added to the dignity of this prestigious building. She was more impressed, though, with the numbers of men entering and exiting the many elevators.

"Hmm," she thought, "lots of opportunities here."

She went up to the third floor, walked down a short corridor until she came to a door marked "Commissioner Timothy Bennet."

Entering, she glanced at the dozen women bent over their computers, then approached the desk of the Office Manager, Mrs. Johnson, who looked up and said, "Yes?"

Tiffany swept her hair back, gave a whinnying laugh which displayed an inordinate number of large teeth, and said, "I'm like here for the interview for Personal Assistant."

Mrs. Johnson gazed at her dumbfounded, she couldn't recall a more unsuitable applicant. Attractive, she thought, in a cheap sort of way, though the legs, she had to admit, were magnificent. With her long legs, large teeth, that whinnying laugh, and her irritating habit of tossing her mane of hair, she bore a faint resemblance to a horse.

She took the file handed to her.

"Er, yes," she said, "take a seat on that bench."

She looked through Tiffany's resume. One year at a Community College studying cosmetology, eighteen months as a hostess at Big Ben's Bar and Grill, one year behind the perfume counter at Bling's Department Store and two months at some lawyer's office. "Ms. Horseley's work was adequate," was the lame recommendation.

Well really, thought Mrs. Johnson, what a nerve applying for this job. I must get rid of her.

She closed the file, but as she rose to her feet to tell the creature that the vacancy had been filled, the door to the Commissioner's office opened and Timothy came towards her. How she revered this man, and how fortunate she felt at being chosen to work for him. There had been fierce competition for this job, not only because of his good looks, but also for his heroism and the gentleness and consideration with which he treated everyone. Mrs. Bennet she loved equally. She looked forward to her twice monthly visits to the office, but as the Commissioner had told her, his wife was writing a book and wouldn't be visiting for some time.

"Well, Mrs. Johnson," he said, handing her two files, "I think these two look promising, we'll put them on the short list."

"I agree, sir. Their résumés are excellent."

Just then he glanced up and saw Tiffany sitting on the bench. His jaw dropped at the sight of those legs.

"Er, um, Mrs. Johnson, who is that?"

"Oh the last applicant, but she's most unsuitable. I was just about to tell her that the position has been filled."

"Well, seeing that she's taken the trouble to come in, I still have time to interview her."

He went back into his office.

Mrs. Johnson handed the file to Tiffany.

"The Commissioner will see you now."

Tossing her head she slithered into his office. She turned to close the door, giving him a good view of her well-developed nether region.

"Ah yes, Ms. Horseley," he ushered her to an armchair, and as she seated herself, he caught a whiff of her perfume. It was cloying, strange and slightly unpleasant.

She glanced around the large room, the impressive desk, the paneled walls, the tall windows looking onto a courtyard. This office and its occupant exuded power, a power she had always dreamed about: attaching herself to an influential and a (hopefully) rich man.

As he sat down opposite her she crossed her legs, confident in the knowledge that they would work their usual magic. She wriggled in the chair, causing her skirt to ride up, exposing two more inches of toned smooth thighs.

"Um, Ms. Horseley," he said barely glancing at her résumé, though one word caught his eye, "I see you were an athlete in high school."

"Oh I'm still an athlete. I train at the track at the city high school every Saturday afternoon, doing laps and like that. I also lift weights and do push-ups."

"Interesting," he watched fascinated as she tossed her head, then raked her fingers with their red painted (false) nails through her hair. "Why did you leave your last job?"

"It was like boring, stuck all day with those files. I'm more of a people person."

"Yes," he said, "that's what's needed in this job, someone who likes people and can deal with them."

Mrs. Johnson closed the last file and sighed. It had been a busy day. She glanced at the clock and couldn't believe her eyes. The Commissioner's interview with that creature had been going on for over half an hour; none of the other interviews had lasted for more than ten minutes. His door opened.

"Well, Mrs. Johnson, I've decided to give Ms. Horseley a month's trial. After that, we can decide whether she'll join our team. Please have the forms ready for her to sign in the morning."

Mrs. Johnson was aghast. She looked at the broad shoulders and long legs, and thought, team? What team? The football team?

Tiffany smiled triumphantly as she strode through the office. She thought, what a middle-aged frump, with her baggy suit, sensible shoes and hairdo left over from the '80's. She waved to the friend who had given her the tip about the vacancy and a thumbs-up sign.

On her way home her mind was filled with the plans she had for the seduction of the Commissioner—it should be like a walkover.

Meanwhile back at the house, Elizabeth was struggling with several chapters of the book. There was more research to be done, much more than she'd anticipated. She'd have to spend a good portion of the next month in the library, tracking down obscure references, and the names and history of the early Board members. She felt guilty at her neglect of her darling Timothy, but thank goodness his work would keep him busy.

Chapter Seventeen

Tiffany's Bold Invitation

Timothy was feeling restless. The coming of spring always had this effect on him. Usually at this time of the year he and Elizabeth would spend every spare minute in the garden. At night they would have social engagements either at home or at restaurants. But this year was different. Elizabeth was so immersed in her writing, their social life had been curtailed.

"Just another month, my darling, and then we'll be back to normal."

Without her he felt at a loose end. She filled his life with joy, activities, discussions and plans for their future.

He stood staring out of the window at the courtyard where he could see tulips were about to bloom. His 5 o'clock appointment had been canceled; he could go home and make a start on weeding the back border. His nostrils twitched. It was that strange perfume his Personal Assistant wore.

He turned to find her standing behind him, her shrewd eyes on a level with his.

"I'll put these last two files on your desk."

He was looking at the small roses tattooed on her upper arms.

"Um, those tattoos, do they signify anything?"

"Oh, I had them done just for fun. I've got like two others," she added.

Before he could stop himself, he said, "Where?"

"Wouldn't you like to know," she said coyly as she took a step towards him. "They're like in a surprising place."

"Well, yes, um, I think I'll be going home now."

"Oh your 5 o'clock has been canceled hasn't it? Why don't you meet me at Randy's Bar, you can have a drink there. They also have complimentary appetizers. A drink would relax you after your busy day."

"Randy's Bar? Where's that?"

"It's a couple of blocks from here. I meet my friends there a couple of times a week, and on Fridays it's like lively, everyone's having fun, it's like awesome."

Well, he thought, why not. Elizabeth will be coming home late and a drink or two might relax me.

When he left the office, he'd decided he'd rather go home. But then as he passed Randy's Bar, he could hear the pounding music through his open window. Crowds of young people were milling around outside. On an impulse he turned the car and valet parked.

He pushed his way through the excited revelers, and as he entered the club he saw Tiffany at the long bar surrounded by girls who all looked the same: their long blonde hair constantly being tossed back. Two of them sported tattoos on their arms.

Tiffany slid off her stool. "Commissioner, let me introduce you."

He said, "Tiffany," and this was the first time he'd spoken her name, "seeing that this is a social occasion, call me Timothy."

"Great, girls, make way for Timothy."

"Hi, I'm Brittney."

"Hi, I'm Courtney."

They made room for him. Young men were circling the bar assessing their prospects for their evening mating entertainment.

After two shots of vodka and half a dozen of the strange-tasting appetizers, he started to quite enjoy himself.

At 9 o'clock Tiffany said, "We're all going to Shooters."

"What's that?"

"It's a strip club. The girls there are like awesome."

"I haven't been to one of those clubs for years."

She laughed, her large teeth glistening.

"You'll find it's quite different from your day. I'll come in your car, then you can drop me back at Randy's afterwards."

At first he was shocked at the explicit moves and gyrations of the strippers, especially when they removed their scanty clothing including their thongs.

"Weren't they like great? Sometimes I can book them for private performances at my apartment. Quite a few people come to watch," Tiffany said.

As she was getting out of the car she said, "Why don't you come tomorrow afternoon and we'll do a few laps at the high school track?"

He agreed to pick her up at her apartment.

When they arrived at the track the following afternoon, there were quite a few athletes doing laps.

"Aren't they like great? We all like to keep fit. They're training for the triathlon," she said stripping off her sweats, "next year I want to try out."

He gaped at the tiny elasticized pants which hugged her like a second skin, and the matching abbreviated bra. Her rather thick waist rippled with muscles.

He found it difficult to keep up with her. He soon lagged behind watching her powerful legs pounding ahead of him. He was breathless after one lap. She, however, seemed unaffected. She dropped to the ground and did ten push-ups.

After another twenty minutes of strenuous exercises, she said, "Come up to my apartment and have a glass of wine before you go home."

While she went to shower, he searched for a glass in the messy kitchen; the sink full of unwashed mugs and glasses, cardboard plates cluttering the counters. He found a plastic glass, poured the wine then drank it off quickly. He was unbearably thirsty. He poured another glassful and had finished half of it while glancing at a brochure that had caught his eye.

"Guys and Gals," proclaimed the title and underneath, "Toys For the Adventurous, Satisfaction Guaranteed!"

When he looked up she was standing in the doorway. She wore an unbelted robe. She held out her hand.

"Come with me," she said, giving her whinnying laugh.

He went willingly to his doom.

***

It was after midnight when he arrived home. Elizabeth was asleep. He switched off his bedside lamp, undressed and collapsed on the bed. He was exhausted.

It was his snoring that woke her at 3:00a.m. She sat up.

"Timothy, Timothy," she shook him trying to stop that awful noise.

He grunted, turned over, then after a few minutes started snoring again.

She sniffed. There was a strange, unpleasant perfume she couldn't identify.

"That smell," she thought. "Must be from when he'd showered at the gym. He must have used that cheap cologne afterwards."

While they were having breakfast, she said, "Did you have a good workout darling? Maybe you overdid it, you must have been exhausted, that's why you were snoring. I couldn't wake you up." She giggled. "You were making so much noise you could have woken the dead."

Alan came up from the basement.

"That smells good Mom; I'll also have two eggs."

He and Timothy chatted while she prepared his food.

"Aunt Jennifer's picking me up. We're all going hiking. She'll drop me back at school."

"Good, darling, don't forget to take all your books. Daniel called this morning, he's through to the finals."

Later Elizabeth said, "Darling, I'll be at the Gardens until late this afternoon. I thought we'd have a bite to eat at that new pizza place on Main Street."

"Oh, er," he said, "I'm going to the gym again, and then I might meet the boys afterwards. And by the way, I'll be late on Wednesday night, we're having a strategy meeting."

"Oh, I'm disappointed. I hear the pizzas are excellent, but never mind, we'll go another time. But," she added, "aren't you overdoing it with another workout? And now a late night meeting as well. I worry about you, my love."

It was again close to midnight when he arrived home. His head was in a whirl. The strippers' performance in Tiffany's apartment was something he'd never before experienced.

Chapter Eighteen

An Unsavory Revelation

Before he had met Elizabeth, Timothy's liaisons had never lasted for more than two weeks. His dalliance with Tiffany followed the same pattern. His interest at the end of two weeks was starting to wane. Even the sight of those magnificent legs failed to arouse him. He was finding her aggressive approach tiring and unappealing. The paucity of her vocabulary matched her I.Q., which he estimated couldn't be much above eighty. She managed, however, to do her job with reasonable efficiency.

But he continued his visits to her apartment on the nights the strippers were available. By the end of the third week, he had become bored with them too. He found their gyrations and antics ridiculous, the cacophony of the music monotonous and deafening.

"I'm not coming to any more performances," he told her at the end of the fourth week.

"Oh but you must see the Asian strippers," she said, desperate to pique his curiosity. "They'll be here for only two days, then they're moving on to Denver."

"Asian strippers, hmm, well maybe I'll come and see them."

"Great, I'll book them for next week."

But Tiffany was more shrewd than Timothy gave her credit for. If all else failed, she had a final plan from which he would be unable to slip from her grasp.

Elizabeth had finished the book. She took the manuscript to the Gardens for a final proofreading and editing. What a relief! She had, she felt, done an excellent job. To celebrate her freedom, she stopped at the Bagel Shop for coffee and a pastry. She was delighted to see John coming in the door.

"Oh John, come and join me, I want to hear all about the wedding."

"Elizabeth, it was great, and I know Penny's written to you, but I want to thank you again for your generous gift. We'll put it to good use. We've missed seeing you at the office, but Timothy says you've almost finished the book, so I hope we'll see you tomorrow night at the Chief's dinner."

"Yes, I'm looking forward to getting back to my old routine. Finishing the book is like a weight off my shoulders."

"By the way," John said, "we missed seeing you last Tuesday at Randy's Bar. Some friends took us there, but we left early, not our scene, too much noise and all those young people." He laughed, "Penny and I are getting too old for that sort of thing. We looked for you when we saw Timothy at the bar with a crowd and his Personal Assistant, Tiffany Horseley, but it was such a mob scene, you must have been standing at the back."

She nodded thoughtfully, "Yes I must have been at the back. I'm also sorry I missed you."

Driving home, she thought, "Last Tuesday, but that was the night Timothy had his evening meeting. Very odd."

The following morning as he was leaving for work she said, "Try and come home a little earlier. We don't want to be late for Jennifer's party."

He looked surprised.

"Jennifer's party? I'm sorry darling, I've got an important meeting tonight."

"Now Timothy," she said firmly, "I've been looking forward to this party. All our friends as well as David will be there."

"Okay, but we might have to leave a little early."

Elizabeth was feeling happy. She was wearing a new dress with petticoat straps, her hair falling in soft waves to her shoulders. She was looking forward to the stimulating and animated conversation that was always a feature of Jennifer's parties, and of course, there was the added joy of seeing David again.

At the dinner table she noticed that Timothy kept glancing at his watch. He'd spoken very little to David, with whom he usually enjoyed long conversations. As dessert was being served, he leaned over to Jennifer and asked if he could use the phone in the study.

Some instinct, was it intuition, caused Elizabeth to stand up and whisper to Jennifer, "Some of my straps are coming loose, can I use your bedroom?"

She closed the bedroom door and sitting on the bed quietly lifted the receiver.

"But sweetie, why are you so late? I'm sitting here all alone, it's like weird, everyone's having fun at Randy's and I'm just like sitting here."

"Tiffany, I told you I'd be late. You go on to Randy's, I'll meet you there. Did you book the Asian strippers?"

"Yes, and some other people are also coming to my apartment. Have you spoken to your wife about the divorce?"

"What do you mean?" He sounded puzzled.

"You said you were going to get a divorce so that we could get married. You told me that on Valentine's night. You remember you sent me all those red roses."

He laughed uneasily, "I must have been drunk. I don't remember anything of the sort."

"Well you did," her voice was shrill. "Those people who were there heard you. Besides I've already told everyone at

Randy's and all the girls at the office, so you can't get out of it now."

"Tiffany, you're talking nonsense, I'm not discussing this with you now." After she'd replaced the receiver, Elizabeth sat for several minutes breathing unevenly.

"Timothy, Timothy, what have you done, oh my God."

She stood up and walked unsteadily to the glass doors leading onto the bedroom terrace. It would be impossible for her to go back into the dining room in her agitated state.

She went out onto the terrace and sat down on a bench. She was shivering from the shock of what she'd heard.

David came out onto the dining room terrace. He strolled towards the swimming pool, then saw her.

"Elizabeth, why on earth are you sitting here? Jennifer's serving the dessert."

She put out her hands, "David, help me. Please help me. I'm in such trouble." She was sobbing, "It's Timothy. He's so gullible."

"Elizabeth, calm yourself, what is it?"

She told him. He shook his head in disbelief. He put his arm around her.

"Oh my God, the bloody fool, what has he got himself into? Look you're shivering my darling. I'll get your jacket and a stiff drink. When you go back inside, tell Jennifer you feel you're getting the flu, that you're sorry to have to leave early, then we'll go back to my apartment. We'll have to discuss a plan that will save your marriage and Timothy's career. He has worked too long and too hard to have it destroyed by this vicious, ambitious woman."

Holding her hands he pondered, if she has already started spreading rumors, it'll be a matter of time before everyone in the building hears about it, including the Chief Commissioner.

He hurried inside.

A few minutes later Timothy came out onto the dining room terrace and came over to her and said, "Elizabeth darling, why are you sitting here alone?"

"I wanted some fresh air," she avoided looking at him.

"Well, um, I have to go to this meeting. I've apologized to Jennifer and she quite understands. I'll take you home and then go on to the meeting."

"I'm staying here, you go to your meeting," she said dully.

"Uh, how will you get home?"

"With David, he'll look after me."

She turned her head aside when he tried to kiss her, then looked at him.

"Yes you run along to your meeting."

He was taken aback at the expression in her eyes. He'd never before seen her look at him like that.

As he drove to the bar, he became uneasy, thinking of her strange behavior, that cold look in her eyes.

When he arrived at Randy's his uneasiness had turned to alarm. His interest in seeing the Asian strippers had disappeared. At the bar he said to Tiffany, "I'm not staying, I have to get home."

"What," she squeaked, sweeping her hair back from her face. "What about the Asian strippers? You'll love their performance. They've come all the way from like Bangkok or Haiti or whatever. They're going on to Denver tomorrow."

"They can go to Timbuktu and the sooner the better. I'm going home."

"Timbuk who? Is it in California?"

"Yes," he said. "It is."

All the lights were still on at home, but where was Elizabeth? He undressed, put on his robe, made a cup of tea, then went into the study. He would work on the investigation report he'd brought home. It was a disturbing case. One of his best officers had been accused of sexually assaulting a prostitute. He sifted through the contradictory statements, the lies of witnesses; all this obfuscation would make it a difficult case to defend. He worked steadily for nearly two hours, marking the salient points, until he felt he would be able to present a coherent case to the lawyers who would defend the officer.

It was nearly midnight. Where was Elizabeth?

All this time Elizabeth had been sitting with David in his apartment. Holding hands, they discussed what course of action to take in order to avert what could become a national scandal.

"Elizabeth, I don't want you to think I'm making excuses for Timothy, but you know men."

She said wearily, "I know David. These things happen, but I want you to know that Timothy has been faithful to me ever since we met. He's always been truthful, but I've always known how gullible he is. I've tried to protect him. If only I hadn't been so involved with the book, I would've seen immediately what was happening. Of course I will forgive him, what I can't forgive is that my good name will be besmirched, my marriage discussed in cheap bars. I feel humiliated. I realize Timothy wasn't aware of this, that's why I say he's gullible and too trusting."

"Darling, don't blame yourself. Men are weak, and presented with the temptations this woman offered, very few men would have been able to resist. Remember, Timothy's love for you is unshakeable, and I'll use every resource I have in order to thwart this evil woman."

"Oh David, there's this dinner tomorrow night. I can't face it."

"You must and you will face it. In fact you must go into the office tomorrow, be calm, act as if nothing is wrong, my sweet, keep a stiff upper lip, and keep your eyes and ears open."

The following morning at breakfast, she said, "I have to go into the Gardens tomorrow. I thought I'd pop into your office on my way home."

"Oh Elizabeth, Mrs. Johnson will be pleased to see you, she's missed your visits."

As he was leaving she said, "I see you were working on the report of that police officer. Have you collected all the evidence?"

"Yes," he sighed, "I'm confident the inquiry panel will go through it thoroughly and that they will come to a favorable verdict. It's a terrible thing for a man to think that his career could be ruined."

"Yes," she replied sadly. "There can be nothing worse."

He clasped her in his arms, "Oh Elizabeth, I love you so."

"I know," she said. "And I will always love you."

Chapter Nineteen

An Office Visit

She dressed carefully that afternoon; a navy blue slim fitting skirt, sling back high heeled shoes, a cream top, the short sleeves and neckline trimmed with navy blue and a matching belt cinching her waist. She used more makeup than usual, more mascara and eyeliner.

Mrs. Johnson jumped up when she saw Elizabeth.

"Mrs. Bennet, I can't tell you how happy I am to see you."

Elizabeth was surprised at this unusual emotional welcome.

To her discomfort she heard the whispers and titterings of the employees sitting at their computers.

Mrs. Johnson ushered her into the small alcove next to her desk.

"Oh Mrs. Bennet," she said in a lowered voice, "I'm not happy with the goings-on in this office."

"Yes," said Elizabeth, "I noticed a change in the atmosphere when I came in. There's a girl sitting in the front, where visitors can see her, eating food out of a cardboard container. She was licking her fingers. Another girl behind you is at this moment applying makeup. I'm surprised you haven't reprimanded them."

"Mrs. Bennet, they take no notice of what I say, my authority has been undermined by that..." she paused "...by that Personal Assistant."

"Have you spoken to the Commissioner about this?"

"Oh no, I would never worry him. He has so much important work to do. As Office Manager I'm supposed to see that the office runs smoothly, he relies on me to do so."

"Well," said Elizabeth and patted her hand. "We'll see what can be done. Is anyone with the Commissioner now?"

"No, he had several meetings this morning. That…" words failed her "…that Personal Assistant is with him. Shall I announce you?"

"No thank you."

As she approached the door she became aware of the renewed whisperings and gigglings behind her. Oh the humiliation, a rage such as she had never before experienced suffused her.

"Keep calm, darling, be your natural dignified self." David's words came back to her.

She paused, took a deep breath and opened the door.

He was sitting at his desk, Tiffany bending over him. He jumped up when he saw her, almost overturning his chair.

She smiled grimly and thought, my sweet Timothy, you look like a small boy who's been caught with his hand in the cookie jar.

"Elizabeth," he brushed past Tiffany. "What a wonderful surprise."

Taking her hands he led her to his desk.

"Er, um, Tiffany, this is my wife, Elizabeth."

Elizabeth barely acknowledged the introduction, taking in Tiffany's almost nonexistent skirt (magnificent legs, she noted), the long blonde hair now being flicked back defiantly, and dear God, were those tattoos on her arms?

Elizabeth, her heart aching, gazed up at her husband and smiled radiantly, her dimples in full play.

"Darling, could I have a word with you?"

"Of course."

"In private, if you don't mind."

"Of course, Tiffany would you wait outside?"

She flounced out, every muscle registering indignation. She slammed the door behind her, then sat at her desk seething. It had been a shock to see his wife, who she'd heard was attractive. But she'd imagined her to be a middle-aged frump. No competition for someone ten years her junior. But the woman who'd entered the office didn't seem middle-aged. In fact she looked as though she'd stepped off the cover of Vogue magazine.

Well, she thought viciously, wait until I tell him next week he has a choice: divorce her or else I'll contact the press. That'll wipe the grin off her face. The scandal will be like awesome.

"Timothy," Elizabeth said gently, "you know I would never have the temerity to tell you how to run your office. It's never been necessary. Mrs. Johnson is so excellent, but there are a few things I've seen today that have disturbed me."

"Something's wrong?"

"Well the first thing I saw when I came in was a girl eating food out of a container. I don't think that sight leaves a good impression on dignitaries coming to see you. Another girl was applying makeup at her desk. I spoke to Mrs. Johnson and she says her authority has been undermined by your Personal Assistant who seems to be running the office. If the employees want extra time off, they bypass Mrs. Johnson and go directly to your Personal Assistant. Mrs. Johnson feels she has become redundant. She's not happy."

He was listening intently to her.

"Some of the girls are wearing scanty clothing, including your Personal Assistant. Quite inappropriate, and Timothy— tattoos and clanking bracelets? After all this is an office, not a bar or a brothel. And by the way, since when do you introduce me to an employee as Elizabeth? Surely I'm still Mrs. Bennet?"

Having delivered this coup de grâce, she waited for his reaction.

"Elizabeth, how can you say that? It's just that we have a more relaxed atmosphere."

"Well, my love, I don't approve. This is one of the most important offices in the city. What you want is not a relaxed atmosphere but one of dignity and discipline."

"Elizabeth, I'm shocked to hear all this. Why hasn't Mrs. Johnson spoken to me?"

"Because she doesn't want to worry you."

"Elizabeth, my darling, you're right, you're always right. I'll do something about this immediately."

He picked up the phone, "Mrs. Johnson, would you step in here, and bring your notepad." Sitting in an armchair, Elizabeth nodded to Mrs. Johnson.

Timothy said, "Mrs. Johnson, these instructions come not from me, but from the Chief Commissioner. My name need not be mentioned. I'll leave the wording to you:

1. Starting on Monday a dress code will be in effect in every office. All female employees must have skirts that reach the knees. Blouses or tops to have sleeves.
2. No jewelry other than marriage rings or engagement rings to be worn.
3. No food to be brought into the office, and no makeup to be applied in the office.
4. Only the Office Manager has the authority to decide whether extra time off can be granted. No other employee can make these decisions.

Mrs. Johnson, can you come in a little earlier on Monday morning, so that these instructions are placed on every desk?"

"Yes sir, I'll see to that."

As she went out Mrs. Johnson smiled at Elizabeth and mouthed, "Thank you."

Timothy walked Elizabeth to the elevator. "I'm pleased you straightened that out darling." Her smile as she looked at him was dazzling, "I'll be ready for tonight."

Chapter Twenty

More Bad News

He was waiting in the study when she came in.

He gasped, "Elizabeth you look stunning, I've always loved that dress on you."

It was a deep blue, slightly off the shoulders. From a gold chain around her neck hung a pearl encrusted cross. Her hair was swept up casually on top of her head.

He took her in his arms, nuzzling her neck, inhaling the subtle perfume of English lavender that was part of her bewitching personality. In the car she sniffed. She couldn't identify the perfume, but she recognized the smell that had been on the sheets a few weeks previously.

In the reception room they were surrounded by friends and those eager to meet Elizabeth.

John and Penny came up to her.

"Lovely to see you again, Elizabeth."

John said, "There are a few new employees in Timothy's office, I'll introduce you."

She braced herself for this ordeal.

He guided her to where the girls were standing.

First girl. "Oh Mrs. Bennet, I'm so pleased to meet you, my Mom's a big fan. She's a keen gardener, she's looking forward to reading your book."

Elizabeth smiled warmly and thanked her.

Second girl. "Are those pearls real?"

Elizabeth was taken aback. "Yes they are."

Her smile was less warm.

Third girl. "Your dress, was it expensive? And is that all your own hair?"

Penny gasped at the impertinence of these questions.

"Yes," said Elizabeth. "It is all my own hair. I'm not in the habit of wearing other people's hair."

John moved her along. "And this is the Commissioner's Personal Assistant."

"Thank you John, I've already met her."

As the dinner drew to a close, the Chief Commissioner stood up and said, "Our accountant has given me the final figures for all the benefit galas Mrs. Bennet held for the Police Fund. The total is $200,000."

Everyone clapped as the Chief shook her hand.

Most of the guests had left. As they were waiting for the elevator Elizabeth said, "I have to use the restroom."

As she was about to come out of the toilet, three chattering girls entered.

First girl. "Well don't tell me the Commissioner would divorce such a beautiful woman to marry Tiffany."

Second girl. "Don't you believe that. Tiffany's cleverer than you think."

Third girl. "She told me that next week she's going to give him a choice: either marry her or else she'll reveal everything to the press and that would be the end of his career, and," she added spitefully, "the end to Mrs. Elizabeth Bennet and her pearls. Tiffany's going to write a book. So whatever happens she'll make a lot of money."

They all laughed excitedly in anticipation of a juicy scandal, and still chattering they left the restroom.

Elizabeth leaned her head against the cold tiled wall. Her stomach was churning as feelings of dread, despair, humiliation and bitterness overcame her.

"Oh Timothy, what have you done to me?"

Should she tell him what she'd overheard? No. On second thought, it would be more prudent to say nothing. He might confront Tiffany and precipitate an outburst which David was anxious to avoid. She was frantic with worry as she rejoined Timothy. David, David, she must speak to him. He would know what to do.

On the way home Timothy said, "You're quiet, my love, are you tired?"

"Yes, I'm a bit tired."

When they arrived home she said, "I have to call David."

"But it's so late."

"No, he's waiting for my call."

She went into the study closing the door.

Ten minutes later when she came out of the study she said, "I'm going to San Diego tomorrow with David and two Board members, it's the regional conference."

"Oh no," he was dismayed. "How long will you be there?"

"About four days. I also want to see the family and catch up on all their news."

She kissed him. "Do you mind if I sleep in the guest bedroom tonight? I want to sleep late tomorrow, I'm really exhausted."

As she closed the guest room door, a foreboding of some disaster awaiting him took hold. He slept badly that night.

Shortly after lunch the following day, Elizabeth entered the office.

Ignoring the snickerings, she said to Mrs. Johnson, "If the Commissioner's not busy could you tell him I'm here? I'm going to San Diego for a few days and I want to give him a few last minute messages."

He hurried out and walked her to the elevator.

As she smiled up at him he rejoiced, "Thank God she's back to normal again. I must have been imagining things last night."

"I've left you cold meats and salads in the fridge. And by the way, that strange smell in your car and on our sheets a few weeks ago is the perfume your Personal Assistant wears. She reeks of it."

"Elizabeth, I want to tell you everything, I can explain."

"No Timothy, we'll talk when I get back."

She felt sad going down in the elevator. Her beautiful Timothy, did he have any idea of the cliff edge they were standing on?

She comforted herself with the thought that David would have a plan. David would save them both.

Twenty minutes later Tiffany sashayed into his office.

"Great news, I've just heard your wife is going to San Diego. Are you separated?"

"No Tiffany, she's going to a conference."

"Oh," she was disappointed. "Well we'll have like fun this week. You must come and stay with me."

"No I can't leave the house."

His head was starting to ache. He swallowed a pain pill.

"Well meet me at my apartment. We'll go to Randy's together, though I'll be late I've got to do some shopping."

"Uh huh, maybe."

He worked steadily for two hours on a case of an officer who had responded to a domestic violence call. A man dressed only in his underpants and wielding a sword had attacked the officer who had shot him. Now the relatives of the wounded man were planning a rally. Their intention was to sue the city for one million dollars, citing police brutality; the case was already in the hands of their lawyers.

His head was starting to throb. He couldn't take any more pills on an empty stomach. The cafeteria was closed, so he decided to go to Tiffany's apartment and on to Randy's where he could have a hamburger, which though barely edible was marginally better than the vile appetizers. At least the hamburger would allow him to take two more pills. He would also pick up a few items he'd left in the apartment, a hairbrush and a comb.

Chapter Twenty One

Return to Me

He opened the front door of Tiffany's apartment and was met by the usual musty smell (did she ever open the damn windows?), but a worse smell was in the kitchen/family room. He looked around repulsed. Six or seven cartons of take-out food were scattered about; on the floor, on the couch and on the kitchen counter. The sink was full of unwashed mugs and glasses, magazines and brochures were lying on the floor. An overturned glass of wine had spilled its contents onto the coffee table. He located the source of the smell. It was a carton containing either a fish or chicken stew on which a green mold was spreading.

What a pigsty! Wearily he sat down on an armchair, then jumped up and looking behind him saw that he'd been sitting on a half eaten hamburger. He sat down gingerly on the chair at her desk. This was where she did her "bookkeeping." A crumpled letter had been tossed aside. He smoothed it out and read,

"Ms. Tiffany Horseley,

Several neighbors have complained about the odor coming from your balcony. When we looked onto your balcony, we saw three open garbage bags. When you signed the lease it was made clear to you that no garbage...blah, blah, etc., etc."

A pile of bills was clipped with one of her hair clasps.

He opened the first one which was from Bling's Department Store.

"To Ms. Tiffany Horseley,

$800 Outstanding Balance

We thank you for your initial deposit of $10. However as it is several months since any further payments have been made, we request that you make an appointment with our Accounts Receivable...blah, blah, etc. etc."

The next letter from the City 1st National Bank was the most alarming.

"To Ms. Tiffany Horseley,

Loan Request, $30,000

As your overdraft had reached its limit, we were unable to consider this loan. However as you have since informed us that your employer, Commissioner Timothy Bennet, is willing to stand as your guarantor, we will reconsider this loan. Enclosed are the forms for Commissioner Bennet to fill in and sign. Blah, blah, etc. etc."

Timothy felt as though his head would explode. He tore the letter in half and shoved it into his pocket.

"That...that..." He couldn't think of a word strong enough that would express his outrage.

He went into the bathroom in search of his brush and comb. Passing through the bedroom, he glanced at the unmade bed with its grubby sheets and the pile of unwashed laundry stacked in the corner.

The bathroom counter was cluttered with uncapped creams (anti-wrinkle), unguents (satisfaction guaranteed) oils and several lipsticks. From an opened tube an evil looking substance was oozing into the sink. He found his brush and comb and thrust them into his pocket. He noticed the large bottle of perfume, almost as big as a flagon. This he thought, was the source of Elizabeth's disdain. "Erotica Magnifico" it proclaimed in gold lettering on the front. Underneath was a painting of a naked Indian lady sitting in an awkward position. He looked at the back of the bottle. "Imported From Pakistan."

He heard the front door slam.

Tiffany, carrying several shopping bags, greeted him.

"Whew, it was like chaos at Bling's. I paid cash so I got a 50% discount."

But he wasn't interested in her purchases or her discounts.

"Why is this place in such a mess?"

"What mess? Oh yes it was that party a few nights ago. You missed all the fun, it was like awesome."

"But why haven't you cleaned up?"

"Me," she was indignant, "I don't have time, besides the maid is coming. You're like cranky today. I'm going to change and then we can go to Randy's."

"I'm not going to Randy's. I've got a headache and I think I'm getting flu."

"Suit yourself," she said unsympathetically.

Not long now, she thought, I can't wait to see his face when I tell him he has two choices. Either way I'm going to be in the money.

Thankfully, and for the last time, he closed the door of her apartment. What a hellhole! In the foyer he threw the brush and comb into a trash can.

Driving past Randy's, the pounding of the music reached him through the open window. It matched the pounding in his head. He was appalled that he'd sat in that bar for two weeks listening to the inane conversations of those girls. "A new restaurant, the food was like gross." "They're getting a divorce. She's already sleeping with Bill. She says he's like weird." "30% discount."

Their brazen, graphic descriptions of their and their friends' intimate encounters never failed to shock him.

He reached home and heaved a sigh of relief as he closed the door behind him. What a sanctuary, everything charming and orderly. He opened the fridge, yes, his darling had left him a large platter of sliced beef, ham and his favorite salami. There were two bowls of salad, one of potato the other of pasta. He'd eat before he took two more pills.

Holding a cup of tea he wandered out onto the terrace, surveying the Garden of Eden he and Elizabeth had created. He went down the steps to check on the blue and white border—his gift to her—it would be spectacular for when they held their first summer party. He noticed five containers. They were perennials she wanted added to the long border, also an untagged rose bush. The tips of the plants were wilting. She must have forgotten to water them. He turned on the hose and gave them a good soaking. From experience he knew they would soon perk up. He sat down at the terrace table and thought back to last year's final outdoor party.

"Oh darling," she had said, "I'm going to enjoy this last party. I've asked Mrs. Sanchez and Maria to do the waitressing and the clean up afterwards. All I've got to do is prepare the dinner. It'll be simple, roast leg of lamb, those small potatoes you like, asparagus and a green salad."

How adorable she'd looked in a strapless summer dress, her face flushed with excitement. David and his date, the pretty daughter of one of the Board members, John and Penny and several neighbors were seated at the other table. David, he had noted, seldom took his eyes off Elizabeth.

After thanking and paying Mrs. Sanchez, she came out and said, "I'm putting on a tape of Dean Martin."

"Oh Elizabeth," they had laughed and groaned, "you and that corny old music."

"My sister and I used to watch our parents and their friends dancing at their parties to all that old music, they loved the Big Band and swing music. What fun they seemed to have. I feel nostalgic when I hear that music. It reminds me of our carefree life in South Africa."

She sipped her wine and her eyes were misty, remembering.

"But I also love the romantic songs of Dean Martin too, especially when he breaks into Italian."

"Well, we know how fond you are of Italy," David said indulgently. "You're always talking about planning a trip there." He had sounded wistful.

"It's because I admire the Italian culture; their language, their warmth and above all how much they've contributed to the richness of Western civilization. Just think of their food, their architecture, the brilliance of their engineering."

"Don't forget Mussolini." He loved to tease her.

"Touché," David had said, grinning at him.

"Oh you two," she had laughed ruefully. "You both like to take me down a peg or two. In any case, all cultures have their ups and downs, Mussolini was an aberration."

"But he did make the trains run on time," David added.

"Put the tape on, Elizabeth, and we'll all dance to Dean's music."

How heavenly it had been holding her in his arms.

"Next year we'll be in Italy," he'd said nibbling her ear.

"Sunny Italy," she'd replied. "Maybe I'll fall pregnant there."

Remembering all this, he sighed regretfully. He'd let her down. He'd neglected her this past month. But he'd make it up to her. In the study he put in the Dean Martin tape and the mellifluous sound of Dean's voice followed him into the kitchen.

The words resonated with him, and oh God, what was this feeling again of some impending calamity? Swiftly he returned to the study and switched off the tape. It was making him depressed.

He sat down at the kitchen table and on a page of one of her notebooks made a list of the chores he wanted to do.

1. Discuss Italian trip
2. Decide on guest list for first summer party
3. Plant perennials and weed front border
4. Strip their bed, put on clean linen, open windows
5. Go to Barnes, buy *Jane Austen: Her Life and Letters*

His headache was lifting. He went into the guest bedroom and sitting on the bed looked at the stack of books on the bedside table and on the floor.

Pride and Prejudice by Jane Austen (she was reading it again?)

The Great Railway Bazaar by Paul Theroux

Charles Dickens, American Notes

Moon Tiger by Penelope Lively

A Good Man In Africa by William Boyd

Under My Skin by Doris Lessing

An *Atlantic Monthly* magazine had several pages marked. She'd probably wanted him to read the article.

The bed looked so inviting, the pillows plumped up and the comforting smell of lavender wafting from the bathroom, enticed him to sleep here.

He undressed, sank down on the bed, covering himself with two mohair blankets. He picked up *Pride and Prejudice*, and began reading it for the second time in two years.

When he looked at his watch he was surprised to see it was after midnight and he was well into chapter seven of the book. He switched off the light and snuggling down under the warmth of the blankets, slept.

He woke up the following morning feeling refreshed. His head was clear. He was eager to start the day. He worked all day in the garden, and feeling tired, had an early night, finishing the book, which made him laugh aloud at the comical characters.

On Sunday morning, having stripped their bed and made it up with clean linen, he decided to go to his house. He hadn't been there for a few months.

"Oh Commissioner, how good to see you."

How lucky he was to have such a good tenant.

"Mrs. Bennet was here last week and when I told her my back was playing up, she dug up the bed, went to the nursery and came back with all these pansies which she planted so we'll have a good spring show."

"Some of the paint needs touching up," he said, "I'll be back with my handyman and we'll paint anything that needs doing."

It was late afternoon when they finished. He sat on the bench she'd given him for his birthday, under the flowering pear tree Ted had expertly pruned. The house was charming with all the changes Elizabeth had recommended, one of the nicest in the neighborhood.

"Don't be tempted to sell your house," she had told him, "one day this area will be valuable."

"Why, what makes you say that?"

"Because these houses are solid and well built. Also the proximity of this area to the city and the University will make it desirable," she replied.

On Sunday night he called John.

"How about getting together for a hamburger?"

John laughed, "We're all meeting at your old precinct's pool room, join us. The guys will be thrilled to see you, and the girls are going to an early movie, they'll be bringing hamburgers and French fries."

How happy he was to see them all. These were his people; decent, loyal and hardworking.

On Monday morning he called Mrs. Johnson and told her he was taking the day off. He asked her to deliver the file on his desk to the Chief. He wanted him to look it over and to make sure he hadn't overlooked anything before sending it onto the lawyers.

"Yes sir," she said, "I'll take it up myself, and there were quite a few sour faces in this office when everyone read those new instructions."

"Good," he laughed, "I'll see you in the morning."

Elizabeth called an hour later.

"Elizabeth, I've missed you so much. Why haven't you called sooner?"

"We've been busy." Her voice sounded tired and strained, "I wanted to tell you we're coming back sooner. There's a storm brewing and David wants to fly out before it gets here."

"Great," he said. "Darling, I've been so busy. I planted those perennials and I cleaned up all the beds. The garden looks wonderful."

"Oh Timothy, that's so helpful, thank you," her voice sounded warmer and stronger. "In the freezer you'll find a container marked Beef Stew, take it out in the morning and leave it on the counter, I'll warm it up for our dinner."

***

San Diego.

On Monday morning David called his lawyer in Hamilton City. He was a close friend and the head of the firm Pilkington and Associates.

"Robert?"

"David, good to hear your voice. What's up? Anything I can do?"

"Robert, a few friends of mine are in a bit of a scrape. I hope you can help. I won't give names. They're very worried. "

"I'm all ears, what sort of scrape and what do you want me to do?"

He told him the scrape they were in and what he wanted Robert to do.

"That should be easy. I'll get my guys working on it immediately," Robert said.

"Thanks Robert, I knew I could depend on you. I'll call you when I get back to Hamilton City."

The following day, Hamilton City.

"Robert, any news?"

"Quite a lot. It seems the party involved has been pimping for Shooters Strip Club, plus holding private exhibitions in her apartment, and making a large profit. My guys visited Randy's Bar and heard a lot of interesting gossip. Do you want us to go ahead?"

"Yes Robert, your people should wait outside her apartment at 5 o'clock."

"Good, David, and tell your friends they needn't worry. We've got everything under control."

Chapter Twenty Two

Too Late For Regrets

He hurried to the door as soon as he heard the taxi arrive. As she opened the door he took her luggage, dropped it to the floor and folded her in his arms.

"Oh Elizabeth, you'll never know how much I've missed you. I have to speak to you to explain."

She stepped back. "Yes, we're going to have a serious talk."

He took her hand and led her outside. "See how I've worked in the garden."

"Yes." She looked sad. "It's all wonderful."

"What's the name of this rose? It wasn't tagged."

"It's called 'Peace.'"

"Peace, yes that's a good name and perfect for this garden. Come inside, I've got a present for you."

In the guest room he gave her the book he'd bought for her.

She unwrapped it and looked at the title.

"Darling, you couldn't have bought me a better gift."

She read the inscription he had written.

"For my darling wife, Elizabeth, who is my greatest treasure, you are the only woman I've ever loved or will love. Your Timothy."

She was silent as tears welled up and dropped onto their hands. She brushed the tears away and led him into the kitchen.

After they'd eaten, she said, "Now for my serious talk. Timothy I've made an appointment with my lawyer in the morning. I'm filing for a divorce."

He felt as though he'd been kicked in the stomach.

"Elizabeth," he gasped. "What are you saying? Is this one of your jokes?"

"No, I'm serious. What I've discovered in the past week has convinced me that I can't continue with this marriage. And now I'll tell you what I overheard in the restroom the night of the dinner."

The color drained from his face. His hands were shaking.

"Elizabeth, how is this possible? Could anyone be so evil?"

"Yes, and ambitious. She was determined to either marry you, or failing that to make money by selling her story to the tabloids. Your career would be ruined, and we would have to stand in front of a national audience while you apologized, made excuses, just like those politicians we've been seeing on T.V. I would never recover from the disgrace. However, if David's plan works, we might be able to avoid this disaster."

"David's plan, what do you mean? David knows about this?"

"Of course. You know I always tell David my problems and he's determined to stop this woman who would ruin your career. Timothy," she said quietly, "I'm going to marry David once the divorce is finalized."

Another kick in the stomach.

"No Elizabeth, I can't believe this, why?"

He was on his knees, his head on her lap, sobbing.

She put her hands on his head smoothing his hair back.

"My darling, it's the only way out for me. Get up sweetheart. I don't want you to kneel in front of me."

She stood up and clasped him in her arms.

"Elizabeth, Elizabeth, I can't live without you. Please forgive me."

"But I do forgive you. The fact that you had an affair I can forgive. What I can't forgive or forget is how my good name has been denigrated. My name bandied about in cheap bars, our marriage discussed and torn apart in those same bars and in your office. I've never known such humiliation and fear as I've experienced this past week. David will rescue me from all this ugliness."

"But I never knew about any of this."

"No, you have such a kind and sweet nature. You could never conceive of anyone wanting to harm you. My darling, you're too trusting."

"Oh Elizabeth, how I regret..."

"Timothy it's too late for regrets."

"So David wins," he said bitterly.

"No you're mistaken. David tried to save our marriage. It was I who made the decision when I realized how serious the situation was and how damaging it would be to my good name. Do you remember several years ago when I unjustly accused you of talking about me? I said then that the only reason I would leave you was if my name was involved in a scandal. Timothy, you've broken my heart."

He groaned, "Yes I do remember, of course I remember."

"Come, let's sit quietly while I tell you what David's plan is. You know how fond he is of you, how much he admires you. He is determined to thwart this woman." Although he was in a state of shock, he listened intently to her.

"The first thing is to remove her from your office before she does more damage, not by firing her, which could cause her to create a scene, but by transferring her to another department. You're to go to the Chief Commissioner first thing in the morning. Tell him because of the economic downturn you've been assessing the expenses in your office and you feel you're overstaffed. Three of the last hired employees could be transferred to other departments."

She continued, "In your office you're to act normally, be polite and agree to any meeting she suggests. Don't worry, you won't be meeting her, especially if David's second part of the plan succeeds."

They spoke for several hours, then Timothy said, "Elizabeth, my darling, come with me."

"No Timothy," she said, "we shouldn't..."

"Please Elizabeth, don't be cruel."

All night they clung to each other. He begging her to stay, making promises, asking for forgiveness; she, soothing him, murmuring endearments, assuring him of her enduring love, till at last, exhausted, they fell asleep.

When he woke up the following morning, he remembered and groaned. He reached for her but she was gone. She'd left a note on the fridge:

"My darling,

Remember: keep calm, act normally, see the Chief as soon as possible. I'll pick you up at noon. Can you take an extra hour off? I want to show you an apartment."

The Chief Commissioner was intrigued with Timothy's proposals for downsizing his staff.

"This idea will certainly save money. You've given me food for thought on how to economize in several other departments. I'll send the letter down to Mrs. Johnson this afternoon. Are you sure she can handle both jobs?"

"Yes Chief, she's very competent."

Tiffany came into his office shortly before noon. He steeled himself to look at her. He struggled to maintain his composure.

"I want to talk to you," she said abruptly. "It's like important, lots of stuff to discuss. Come to my apartment tomorrow."

"Certainly," he said politely. "I'll be there."

While he and Elizabeth were having lunch, he said, "Why are you showing me an apartment?"

"Because that's where you're going to live. Timothy I'm selling the house."

"Oh my God Elizabeth, our garden."

"Darling, if I rent the house, the garden will be destroyed within a year. Tenants would never be bothered with it. The real estate person in our area knows of a couple. They're keen gardeners, who are looking for a house in our area but because they can't afford the high prices, I've decided to lower the price considerably."

"Elizabeth, you're destroying everything we've worked for."

She looked at him reproachfully.

"No I'm sorry darling, you've never destroyed anything. I'm to blame, my stupidity and for a few cheap thrills, I've destroyed our lives. But what about Alan and Daniel?" he asked.

"Alan will be staying with Jennifer for a week, then I'll be going with him to the U.K. and I'll stay there for a few weeks to see that he's settled in his school. Daniel," her eyes filled with tears, "our darling Daniel. While he's on this tennis tour, he shouldn't be distracted. I've told Alan to keep in touch with him, after all, they're almost like brothers."

In the apartment she pointed out the spectacular view of the city.

"You'll be comfortable here. I'm giving you all my furniture, all except the antiques that Hugh inherited from his family. It'll be stored in England until Alan has his own establishment."

"Elizabeth, after dinner tonight..."

"Timothy, I'm not coming back to the house. David leaves for the U.K. tonight and I'm moving into his apartment. I don't want to prolong our agony, and," she added gently, "you won't change my mind." She paused, "Timothy, next year I'll be thirty-six, I want more children."

As he started to protest she held up her hand.

"I'll never feel confident that this will never happen again, and by then I'll be too old to make any changes. With David I'll feel safe."

She put her arms around him, looking at the beautiful face she had loved.

"Timothy, I've always been so proud of you; your keen intellect, your bravery, and your loyalty to your officers. I know that in the years ahead you'll achieve even greater success, and that I will continue to be proud of you and that for five years I was part of your life. Listen to me my sweet, you have given me five years of happiness, more happiness than most people have in a lifetime, and for that we should be grateful."

He knew then that it was hopeless trying to persuade her to stay. Elizabeth had always been cautious, but once she had made up her mind, she would never waver.

Three months later she returned from the U.K. They signed the final divorce papers. She was leaving that afternoon.

They had a last lunch at their favorite restaurant.

As they sat holding hands, she said, "Timothy, I met Daniel yesterday," she blinked away a few tears. "You can imagine how traumatic it was. I went with him to the bank and opened an account in both your names. I know he'll be getting a scholarship for college, but he'll need living expenses. His mother won't be able to help him. Timothy, you'll always guide him and help him. Our darling Daniel who brought us together. He and Alan will keep me in touch with your news, because we'll never be able to correspond with each other. It wouldn't be fair to David."

She held his hand against her cheek and looked steadily into his eyes.

"Even though thousands of miles will separate us, you'll always be in my heart, my brave beautiful lover."

In the foyer she said, "Don't come outside. I'll say goodbye to you here."

Sobbing, she clung to him. Cupping her hands on either side of his face, she kissed him again and again.

She went through the glass doors to the waiting limousine. As it glided away, he thought, what folly had led him into that apartment and into the clutches of Tiffany, that vicious and conniving woman. Those few weeks of entertainment had cost him his happiness, and the loss of the only woman he would ever love. He walked slowly back to his office.

Chapter Twenty Three

Tiffany Receives Some Unsettling News

[Gentle Reader: You, no doubt will be curious as to what is in store for Tiffany, that serpent who slithered into the Garden of Eden and tempted the male. So let us go back to the day several months previously when she had arranged to meet Timothy.]

As Tiffany was about to leave the office, Mrs. Johnson handed her a letter.

"What's this?" Tiffany asked suspiciously.

"It's from the Chief Commissioner."

"Well, I don't have time to read it now."

She put it in her tote bag.

As she neared the entrance to her apartment building, two neatly dressed gentlemen approached her.

"Ms. Tiffany Horseley?"

"Yes," she said impatiently.

"We represent the law firm of Pilkington and Associates. We've been making inquiries into the entertainments you've been holding in your apartment."

"So? It's like a free country, what's it got to do with you?"

"Well it appears that the Asian entertainers you hired are in this country illegally."

"What do you mean?" she demanded shrilly. "They're employed by Shooters."

"Yes, but before you hired them, you should have checked their status. And there are suspicions that they have been involved with drug dealers."

She paled, "But I don't know anything about that. And who told you all this?"

"Several men who attended your entertainments have been told by a friend of yours that you intend exposing them to the press, and making a lot of money in the process."

"Who are they, these men?"

"We're not at liberty to disclose who they are, but they have instructed us to contact the immigration authorities and the police if there's any hint that your intentions are to create a scandal involving them. They are wealthy, powerful men and they will use all their influence to destroy you."

"That's a lie. I've never said I'd do anything like that, and besides those strippers work for Shooters."

"Well that club will also be investigated by Immigration and the police. They would be closed down and you and the club would face a heavy fine and jail time. Have a nice day."

As they were driving off, the first gentleman said to his companion, "Well you certainly scared the bejesus out of her."

The companion called his office.

"Everything went according to plan, sir. You can tell your clients they have nothing to worry about."

Tiffany sat on her still unmade bed, pondering her next move. She was shocked at what those two assholes had told her. Which men could have gone to the lawyers? She could remember very few of them, but it definitely couldn't have been Timothy, who she knew was too discreet to expose himself to a scandal. And who was the friend who had let her down by talking to the men about what she was going to do? It was her own fault, she decided, for boasting about her plans, and the money she would be making. They were envious and jealous. Her finances were shaky. She'd relied on the revenue she collected from Shooters. Now she wouldn't dare go back there.

She opened the letter from the Chief. Transferred to the filing department? Now she wouldn't be able to go back to Randy's Bar, where the news of the loss of her powerful friend as well as her demotion would soon spread. The gigglings and gossiping of those so-called friends would be too humiliating.

Well, she had to hold onto that filing job until something better turned up. She had a restless night, and as a result overslept making her an hour late to the office. Her desk and chair were missing. In their place was a large container with a tropical tree planted in it.

"Where's my desk?" she demanded of Mrs. Johnson, who was watering the tree.

"That desk and chair have been taken down to the second floor," she said mildly. "And I do think this tree will do well in this corner."

"But where am I supposed to sit?" She glared at the girls who were watching her and snickering.

"Didn't you read the Chief's letter?" replied Mrs. Johnson. "You've been transferred to the filing Department."

"I want to speak to the Commissioner."

"He's not in his office. He has meetings in the city for the rest of the week."

Christ, she thought, whichever way I turn I seem to run into a brick wall.

"Where's the filing department?" she asked sullenly.

"It's in the lower basement, but you can't use the regular elevators. They stop at the foyer. You must use the freight elevator which goes down to the basement, and I do think I see buds on this tree," Mrs. Johnson said.

Tiffany stormed out of the office and reaching the lower basement, went up to the counter where Officer Jones was waiting for her.

She was a tall, angular woman with a severe expression. She wore steel-rimmed spectacles and a faint mustache. She had a sharp nose and an even sharper tongue. A retired police officer, she ran her department the way she'd run the recruitment program for women, with discipline and competence.

"You're late," she snapped.

"Yes, I was like getting my stuff," said Tiffany.

"There's a lot to do," the gorgon indicated a trolley laden with files. "You can start with these. The two recruits on the other side are in charge of A-K. You'll be doing L-Z, but be careful you don't confuse the files M and N. If the Chief wants an M or N and they're mixed up, it causes problems, and wastes a lot of time. Do you understand?"

Tiffany, bewildered, felt she'd never heard such gibberish in all her life.

"Yes."

"And," continued the dragon, looking with disfavor at Tiffany's shoes, "you'd better wear sensible shoes. You'll be doing a lot of standing and walking. Your overall is hanging on a hook in the restroom."

And with that she marched back to the counter to give hell to a nervous young recruit who'd misplaced a file.

"What?" fumed Tiffany. "Filing department, freight elevator, and now a fucking overall?"

The overall was an unhappy combination of orange and pink flowers against a green background, and because it was too small for her, the sleeves reached only to her elbows.

Christ I must look like ridiculous, she thought.

In the first hour she broke two fingernails.

Her persecutor materialized behind her.

"You're very slow. Another trolley has just arrived. You won't be able to take a regular lunch break. Ten minutes only because you were so late. I've ordered a sandwich and coffee for you from the cafeteria."

Intimidated, seriously depressed and gloomy, she sat on a bench outside the restroom eating her sandwich. She mulled over her suddenly diminished status.

An hour after lunch she broke another fingernail, and she suspected that one of her hair extensions was coming loose.

She heard a trolley trundling up the corridor.

"Well hi," said Herb Schnauzzer, the Manager of Janitorial Services. He leaned on his trolley which contained mops, brooms, brushes and other cleaning paraphernalia. He looked her over approvingly.

"It's great to see a good-looking woman here instead of that," he lowered his voice, "that dragon."

Grey hairs sprouting from a mole on his chin matched his straggly mustache. He clicked his dentures unattractively.

"This is Harry, my Assistant Manager."

The Assistant Manager was wearing capacious, three quarter length pants, the crotch of which almost reached his knees.

"Hi," he said, smoothing back his ponytail. His nose ring and an overabundance of tattoos on his arms rounded out his unprepossessing appearance.

"We heard you were down here, and Herb and I want to like take you for coffee."

His Adam's apple bobbed up and down excitedly.

Before Tiffany could reply to their kind offer, they heard clumping footsteps approaching.

"What's going on here?" barked the dragon, her nose twitching. "What's all this talking?"

She looked with displeasure at the Manager and his Assistant.

"You're supposed to be upstairs on the third floor fixing those shelves. They've already called down twice and you," she said to the cowed Assistant, "you haven't mopped the floor in the foyer."

Harry hurriedly picked up the stepladder. "Yes Ma'am," he said, tugging at his pants, the crotch of which was almost sagging to his knees. "You betcha."

"No sweat," added Herb.

"What pathetic workers," snorted the dragon. "How they keep their jobs is a mystery."

A voice called from the front counter.

"Anyone there?"

Tiffany hastily moved behind the shelves. She recognized the voice of that handsome Commander who'd been eyeing her in the elevator this past week. She didn't want to be seen in this condition; broken fingernails, hair extension coming loose and this fucking overall. The corn on her small toe was aching.

"Oh Officer Jones," wheedled the Commander, "I've come personally to ask if we could return the files in the morning."

He smiled ingratiatingly, "We've got a meeting..."

"I'm sorry Commander, you know the rules. All files have to be returned by 6 o'clock."

She considered it inconsistent with her dignity to be swayed by blue eyes and an ingratiating smile.

"I thought you could make an exception."

"No exceptions."

Switching off his smile and muttering imprecations, he departed.

At 5 o'clock Officer Jones came to check on Tiffany's progress.

"You're very slow. I thought you'd be finished by now. You'll have to work overtime, and I see you've mixed up some of the M's and N's. Didn't I tell you?"

But Tiffany had had enough. Ripping off the overall, she threw it onto the floor. She rushed into the restroom and collected her bag and purse. Passing the openmouthed dragon she said through gritted teeth, "Fuck you and fuck your files."

But the final insult was still to come.

The freight elevator stopped on the first lower floor. The doors opened to reveal Herb and Harry. His pot belly straining against his overalls, Herb leaned nonchalantly against the open door.

"Great," he said. "We meet again."

"Yes," said Harry, his Adam's apple bobbing up and down. "Me and Herb here was thinking, instead of coffee, maybe we'd treat you to a hamburger at the Hamburger Hangout. There's like a great crowd there, and all the guys want to meet you. My best pal Dwayne, he's just been promoted to Supervisor of the Sewage and Outdoor Litter Removal, really fancies you, and," he added as an inducement, "if we go before 7 o'clock the beer's half price."

He leaned the stepladder against the other open door.

Before she could reply, a navy blue whirlwind clattered down the stairs. When it calmed down it resolved itself into the form of a paunchy Sergeant sporting ferocious eyebrows.

"You miserable asshole," he said, addressing Herb, not Tiffany. "What do you think you're doing holding up the elevator like this?"

The veins in his neck stood out like cords.

"Do you know that there are four officers waiting to bring their files down here? And you," turning to the quaking Harry, "you son-of-a-bitch get that stepladder away from that door."

He was almost foaming at the mouth with rage. His ferocious eyebrows moved up and down. "Get out," he bellowed.

"No problem-o," said Harry hoisting the ladder onto his shoulder, at the same time trying to haul up his pants, the crotch of which was threatening to descend well below his knees.

And so we say farewell to the Manager, Herb Schnauzzer, and his trolley filled with mops, brooms, brushes and other cleaning equipment. And also to Harry, his trusty Assistant Manager bringing up the rear.

As the door of the elevator opened at the foyer, the Sergeant bared his teeth in a mirthless grin and said to Tiffany, "Have a nice day, Ma'am."

She walked or rather limped (fucking corn) through the entrance doors which five weeks previously she had entered with such high hopes.

And so the question of whether Tiffany would have accepted the enticing offer of being treated to a hamburger and a half-price beer at the Hamburger Hangout, as well as an introduction to Dwayne, the recently promoted Supervisor of Outdoor Sewage, will forever remain unanswered.

Chapter Twenty Four

Tiffany In Paradise

After her ignominious ousting from her prestigious job, Tiffany lost no time in finding a new one. She sat on a high stool behind the perfume counter of the Parfum et Cosmetique Boutique. Behind her on the display counter a placard listed the services available:

Coiffures

Facials

Manicures

Pedicures

Plucking

She was on the lookout for a suitable candidate for her next conquest. No more young men, she'd decided. Their wives were too attractive and vigilant. Older men with dumpy wives were to be her target. The clientele here were well-heeled, the women either rich or married to rich men. Bejeweled, botoxed and in cold weather befurred, they flocked into the boutique to be pampered and cured for a few hours of their boredom with spicy gossip.

A frump of a wife wearing an ill-fitting suit and a beehive hairdo came up to her. Her husband, she could see, had a roving eye. They were certainly roving as he looked at her magnificent legs. On the happy side of sixty, he was trim, silver-haired and attractive. Gold watch, she noted, and gold cuff links; always a good sign.

"I'm looking for a gift for my sister," said Martha Dolton, "I want something French."

"Yes, Madam," said Tiffany, turning to the display cabinet behind her, well aware that the husband's eyes were out on stalks as she bent down.

"Well," said Martha looking at all the testers, "I think I'll play it safe with Chanel No.5. What do you think Mark?"

He couldn't have cared less whether it was Chanel No. 5, 10 or 20. His eyes were glued on those legs, and the blonde hair being flicked back.

"Quite right, my dear, better to be safe."

"And what are these bottles?" Martha asked.

"They're the latest anti-wrinkle cream from, like Europe. It's made from the Queen's Bee honey. But they're not for sale. They're, like, samples."

"Oh what a pity I would have bought them all."

"If Madam will wait, I'll ask the manager."

The manager standing behind the display counter smiled, she'd been trying to get rid of that garbage for several months. Here was an opportunity to off-load them.

Tiffany turned back to Martha. "They're our fastest selling line, we're expecting another shipment in a few weeks, but we can let you have them," she said with a whinnying laugh.

"I'll take four, put two of them with my sister's gift, and I want them gift wrapped."

"Certainly Madam, I'll send them down to the gift wrapping department."

"I can't wait. Mark, my dear, would you come back later and pick it up?"

An hour later he returned. Tiffany bent down to retrieve it from the bottom drawer, giving him a good view of her thong.

"What's your name?"

"Tiffany Horseley, but you can call me Tiffany."

He looked at the placard on the counter.

"What's plucking? Is it eyebrows?"

"And other places," she raked her fingers through her hair. "Interesting places."

"Oh, really? And those tattoos, what do they mean?"

"They were just for, like, fun. I've got two others."

"Oh where?" he asked before he could stop himself.

"Wouldn't you like to know," she said flirtatiously.

The following week found him once more at the perfume counter. "I wondered if you'd like to have a drink with me after work. My wife is visiting her sister. She'll be away for five weeks."

"Great," she said. "Meet me at la Femme Bar and Grill, it's around the corner." The women at la Femme were older, more sophisticated and better dressed than those at Randy's. Known as "Cheetahs" they were like their African counterparts, sleek and swift; when they spotted a prey, they were quick to enter into a relationship. The men too were older, but they were wary and wily. Most had several divorces behind them and hefty child support payments. They weren't eager to "commit" or to enter into a permanent relationship.

Mark was enjoying himself sitting with all these lively young people, and the liveliest was sitting next to him.

"Later we're going to Pistol Pete's Strip Club, the girls there are like awesome." (She was giving Shooters a wide berth.) "And I can book them for a private performance in my apartment, are you interested?"

He went willingly to his doom.

A week later, Mark, lying on Tiffany's bed, was studying a brochure she'd given him.

"PARADISE BEACH: THE GLAMOROUS LIFESTYLE YOU DESERVE!"

The photograph depicted attractive people; the girls in thongs, the older men in white pants and navy blue blazers sitting on a terrace overlooking a blue sea and sipping exotic drinks. Several yachts could be seen in the background.

"THIS TOO COULD BE YOUR FUTURE."

"Wouldn't it be great if we could live there?" she said seductively.

Martha Dolton was philosophical when Mark told her he was leaving her.

"Paradise Beach, hmm, that sounds ambitious. But I'll not consider a divorce Mark. There's never been a divorce in our family and besides you'd get very little in a settlement. You know my money is tied up in a trust. I'm disappointed of course at this news, but you've been a good husband and father, and you're an attractive man, so I can understand your wanting to lash out a bit. I'll tell father you're taking a break to write a book, a history of Hamilton City. I'll make sure your salary at the bank will be paid for three months, and of course you have a very comfortable nest egg."

Two weeks later, Mark was sitting on the private terrace of the Paradise Beach Club, the down payment of which had made him gulp. It was well-removed from the public beach where the hoi polloi disported themselves. Surrounded by attractive people, sipping exotic drinks, and with his trophy girlfriend lying next to him, he was content. This was the life!

Tiffany, wearing a new beach outfit, bit into a club sandwich, her third that morning noted Mark (my how that girl could eat), and chatted to the other trophy wives and girlfriends.

Their talk was of shopping, jewelry and yachts, while the men discussed the stock market, mergers and acquisitions.

Every night they ate at an expensive restaurant (Tiffany rarely went into the kitchen in their luxurious apartment), where her favorite items on the menu were lobster, filet mignon and a mélange of tiny vegetables, followed by dessert of either baked Alaska or crepes suzette.

Mark was standing at the bar when a man sidled up to him.

"Hi," he said, looking at Mark speculatively. He had slicked-back hair and an expansive smile which showed more than a full complement of teeth.

"You're new around here."

"Yes, we arrived two weeks ago," said Mark.

"Well, we're guests of the Sanders. I'm sure you've noticed their yacht. It's the biggest in the harbor. Our next stop is the Bahamas. Why don't you join us for an after dinner drink?"

A few nights later as he and his new friend were sitting at the bar, the friend said confidentially.

"I shouldn't be telling you this, but my cousin's brother-in-law is the hedge fund manager at Grabbe, Swindell and Snatcher." He lowered his voice. "He told me this in confidence that A. & C. Conglomerates are going to be taken over by C & A International. You know they've just landed a big defense contract."

Mark didn't know, but he nodded.

"And anyone who buys in now will clean up. But don't say a word to anyone. My cousin's brother-in-law could lose his lob. His bonus last year was over five million dollars."

Mark lay in bed that night reading the A. & C. brochure given to him by his new friend. Although the claims by the company of the profits they had made the previous year strained credulity to the utmost, he had no doubts.

The following morning while Tiffany was consuming a plate of Eggs Benedict with an extra side of ham, he called his broker and placed an order for A. & C. shares.

Two days later, the share price had doubled. His delight was tempered by the annoyance of having been too cautious, he should have bought more.

His new friend was at his usual place at the bar.

"Well pal, we're going to clean up, but I've got even better news. There's talk," he lowered his voice, "that there's a third party interested in A. & C. There could be a bidding war. My cousin's brother-in-law is putting in an order for ten mill."

The following morning Mark was on tenterhooks waiting for his broker to call.

"Mr. Dolton, this is a very large investment in A. & C. You realize it will leave you only $100,000 in your account?"

Within a few days the share price had doubled again. He calculated that with the shares going up every day, he would be a wealthy man.

"We're having a poker game in a friend's apartment," said his new friend, "just small stakes, these guys aren't too good. Why don't you join us?" He added, "Sometimes Lord Marmaduke Swanky from Poshington Manor in the U.K. and his friend Archibald Hetherington-Hetherington join us if they're in town. Do you know them?"

"No," said Mark, slightly intimidated. He had not even a nodding acquaintance with anyone with a double-barreled name, let alone an aristocrat from the U.K. But he felt flattered to be included in this august group. He accepted the invitation and though the stakes were higher than he'd expected, in the first week he was up $500. The second week his luck deserted him and after four sessions he realized to his horror that he had lost in cash over $10,000.

But as his new friend said, "Your shares are worth a fortune. $10,000 is peanuts."

Tiffany enjoyed these sessions. She and the girls had engrossing conversations about shopping and how to inveigle their partners into buying them jewelry. With the share price going up, Mark bought the emerald ring that Tiffany had been eyeing. She felt confident that the matching bracelet would soon follow.

A few weeks later as they were coming down to the terrace, Mark noticed a group of men talking and gesticulating excitedly.

"What's up?" he asked.

"The market's crashing, it's already down 30%."

"Good God, what's the reason?"

They shrugged and said it was a "correction," but they looked uneasy.

"Even the blue chips are plunging," another man said gloomily.

"Well you know what the saying is," a man in a yachting cap said. "When the police raid the brothel, even the piano player is arrested."

They all laughed, but they looked concerned.

Despite the assurances of the Chairman of the Stock Exchange that this was just a "correction," and investors shouldn't panic, the shares continued to plunge. Mark saw with alarm that his shares had lost nearly 40% of his profits.

That night at the bar, his new friend was reassuring. "Just a correction," he said, though his smile was less expansive.

But the correction turned into a rout, as investors continued to sell. All of his profits had disappeared and also a large chunk of his capital. An ominous headline in the *Wall Street Journal* reported that A. & C. was being investigated by the S.E.C. for fraudulent dealings. Several hedge fund managers from Grabbe, Swindell and Snatcher had been arrested. This news caused the share price to plunge almost to nothing. Mark had lost almost all his capital. That night at the bar he looked for his new friend.

"Oh," said the bartender, "they've all gone. The Sanders yacht set sail this morning."

Tiffany went down as usual to the terrace, flashing her new ring and wearing a recently purchased beach outfit. Mark stayed in the apartment assessing his disastrous situation.

He went to their private gym and canceled their membership. He went to the department store and canceled Tiffany's line of credit. His final stop was at the club's office where he asked for a refund of his membership fee.

"We can only refund you half," said the manager coldly. He possessed none of the attributes of empathy and tact so necessary in an employee. He dismissed Mark with a wave of his hand.

Back at the apartment, clutching the *Wall Street Journal* and the calculator, he pondered on how else he could economize. He called the maid service and canceled them too.

Chapter Twenty Five

How The Mighty Have Fallen

Mark hustled Tiffany past the club's terrace and onto the public beach where hordes of overweight parents and their crying children were frolicking on the sands. A contingent of senior citizens had taken possession of all the chairs and umbrellas, so they had to sit on their towels.

"Why are we sitting here with all these old people," she whined, glaring at several octogenarians who were gaping at her (she'd become careless with the maintenance of her bikini line).

He'd tried to explain to her the market crash, the loss of his fortune, the need to economize. He looked with bitter regret at the ring on her finger.

"But what about my club sandwiches," she wailed. "All they've got here," she gestured at the concession stand manned by a harassed looking teenager wearing a baseball cap turned backwards, "are hot dogs and doughnuts."

He smiled grimly at the wrinkled item she'd just taken a bite out of. That hot dog was surely a leftover from the Carter Administration. No more lobsters, filet mignon or fancy desserts. At the rate she'd been spending, he'd have soon gone bankrupt.

For two days he sat with the *Wall Street Journal* and his calculator musing at how he'd believed that the cousin's brother-in-law had information straight from the horse's mouth, information that had proved to be inaccurate. That night he threw the A. & C. brochure into the garbage, consigning it to the oblivion it so richly deserved.

To add to his irritation, his legs were peeling. His tan had never gone beyond several red patches. Even his goddamn toes were peeling.

The following day as they were lying on their towels Tiffany said, "Why are you always fiddling with that calculator thing. You're, like, getting on my nerves. And where are we going to eat tonight?"

"The Eezie Dining Restaurant. We'll take advantage of the Early Bird."

"What," she burst out indignantly. "That's the fourth time this week."

"I know how you enjoy the food there," he said sarcastically. "You can order your favorite lobster."

At 4 o'clock they entered the Eezie Dining Restaurant (Early Bird, Seniors Welcome) and were seated at a long table where their fellow diners were senior citizens from a retirement home. He and Tiffany were an unwilling captive audience as they were forced to listen to a recitation of their fellow diners' activities.

A sprightly woman who seemed to have applied her lipstick with an unsteady hand, said, "So I said to her, are you blind? Can't you see it is a mole, I want the doctor to see…"

"…Then I put the eye drops in little Mitzi's eye," said another woman with blue hair, "and she started howling. I said to the vet…"

The slightly deaf man sitting opposite Mark had been biding his time, waiting for a break in the conversation. He adjusted his hearing aid and lower dentures and bellowed.

"I don't know anything about voles, but I'm here to tell you Jimmy Carter never would have lost that election, only he was messing around with them Eye-Ranians, and," he added, "Elvis lives. Why my cousin saw him in Hank's Convenience store buying a Big Gulp!"

He had a hacking cough which was rich-sounding and productive.

"Christ," thought Mark. "Is this the level I've sunk to? Listening to drivel and eating this vile food?"

He recalled with nostalgia Martha's dinner parties, the sophisticated conversation, the delicious food. What in God's name was he doing here? He hated this place, Paradise Beach, the unrelenting sun, the humidity, and those palm trees. He longed to be back in Hamilton City with its crisp air, the trees starting to turn, and soon there'd be a dusting of snow on the mountains.

Tiffany was bleating again. "Mark, this pasta is, like, gross."

He ignored her. He found everything about her revolting.

The following day he managed to get two chairs, and while he was studying the share prices (another disastrous day) he felt someone looking over his shoulder, reading the headlines.

"The market's going down the toilet," chortled the old codger. "Lots of people going to lose their shirts, heh, heh." He smiled, revealing a set of gleaming dentures.

Still chuckling at the thought of all those shirts being lost, he moved over to get a better view of Tiffany's carelessly maintained bikini line. Mark didn't care, her legs had long ago lost their appeal.

She was thinking, crap, I've landed myself with another dud. But that restaurant there, lots of men from the yachts are going in there. I'll get changed and go and apply for a job there.

She stood up. "I'm going to, like, do some shopping."

Mark had a raging thirst. He went up to the concession stand. A seriously unattractive group of senior citizens wearing shorts and abbreviated tops converged on the stall, elbowing him out of the way.

"Irma," screeched one across the counter, "I'm having a hot dog and a doughnut."

"No thanks," a grating voice replied from the other side, "I'm watching my figure."

As they waddled away, the veins on their legs looking like a relief map of the Himalayas, Mark noted that several of them had rear ends only slightly smaller than Rhode Island.

"Who are those women?" asked Mark.

"They've got like a club, S.W.A.T & S.E, it stands for Seniors with Attitude and Self Esteem, they're very aggressive. You don't want to be here when they do their yoga exercises. Anyway, I'm off to Aspen as soon as I save enough money, I'm outta this hellhole." He added, "I hear the surfing in Aspen is, like, awesome."

Mark said, "There's no surfing in Aspen, lots of snow and skiing."

"Whatever, I never was too good at geography," he said fiddling with his nose ring.

Christ, thought Mark, I can't take much more of this.

He hurried to the apartment and sitting on the bed placed a call to Hamilton City. He almost sobbed with relief when Martha answered.

"Oh Martha. I want to come home."

"Of course Mark," she said kindly, "I'm pleased to hear from you. I'll tell father you've finished the outline for your book on Hamilton City, and that you'll be back at your desk in a few days."

He immediately called the airline and booked a single, one-way ticket to Hamilton City. Then he called for a taxi. He hastily packed his suitcases, happily throwing out all the recently purchased flowered shirts and leisure wear onto the pile of Tiffany's unwashed laundry. And so as the sun sets slowly in the West, we take leave of Paradise Beach and its exclusive club, and our two protagonists....

Mark Dolton, anticipating a return to a well- ordered, dignified life, a rise in the stock market, and perhaps a new set of golf clubs.

And Tiffany Horseley, dreaming of a future with a rich yachtsman in a navy blue blazer with brass buttons, shopping malls, jewelry stores and a never-ending supply of hair extensions.

Chapter Twenty Six
Part Two

Timothy's New Life

For two months after Elizabeth's departure, Timothy was in a state of shock. Mourning her loss, he became withdrawn, taciturn and antisocial. He took on extra assignments, working long hours to avoid going back to his apartment. He had lost weight, the scratch meals he bought from the deli he found unappetizing.

Every night he sat at the table looking out at the city lights, playing all the tapes they had loved and danced to; the melodies and words echoing in his head even when he slept.

He climbed out of this Slough of Despond with the arrival of Alan's letter:

"Dear Commissioner Timothy,

My apologies to you for not saying goodbye to you personally. As you can imagine my life was pretty chaotic for a few weeks, however I've settled down at my school (it helps that my cousins are at my school) and having the family living nearby also helps.

I miss you and Hamilton City. I'll never forget your kindness to me and the good times we had for five years. I also miss Daniel and have written to him. We were almost like brothers, perhaps we'll meet again soon. Mom says I must keep you informed and I hope you'll write to me often (if you have time) and let us know how you're getting on. We're all so proud of you. By the way, Mom is expecting a baby. She looks well and is as active and as beautiful as ever.

Your affectionate friend,
Alan."

With an ache in his heart he read the last sentence several times. So she hadn't wasted time getting pregnant. Oh Elizabeth, that could have been our baby. He thought of how disappointed she'd be if she could see him now, hollow-eyed and wallowing in his misery.

He gathered up all the tapes and put them in the chest where he kept all the letters and memorabilia of their years together. That night he went to a good restaurant and enjoyed the first proper meal he'd had in months.

Two days later he had a meeting with the Chief.

"Everything going well? Any news of Mrs. Bennet? You said she'd returned to England. When will she be back?"

"She's not coming back, Chief. She's decided to stay in the U.K. to be near her family. She asked me to join her there but that of course was impossible. I could never leave my work here. We've had an amicable divorce, and we will always love and respect each other."

This was the prepared speech Elizabeth had told him to deliver. She had said she'd be writing to all their friends, but advised him to say as little as possible.

"I'll soon be forgotten Timothy, nobody is indispensable."

"No Elizabeth," he had replied. "Everyone whose life was touched by you will always remember you."

The Chief stammered, taken aback, "I'm deeply sorry to hear this. Mrs. Bennet was our most loyal supporter. She will always be remembered for her kindness and dedication to law enforcement."

The set lips and stern expression on Timothy's face did not encourage further questioning. The news filtered through the building, but the cause of the divorce remained a mystery.

When she heard the news Mrs. Johnson wept.

"Oh Mrs. Bennet, how I loved you, and how I will miss you."

When she received a letter from Elizabeth, praising her for her devotion to Timothy and asking her to continue helping him in his work, she wept again.

As the news reached the wider world, the socialites realized that here was the most eligible bachelor in Hamilton City; handsome, heroic and in a powerful job. Invitations to parties, galas and charitable events trickled in, then became a flood and within six months Timothy was unable to cope with all the invitations. His needs too were being met satisfactorily. He chose his partners carefully. They were older attractive women who were married to rich men. Above all they were discreet. They had no wish for a scandal or a divorce which would disrupt their comfortable lives....

In the third year of living in the apartment, Timothy began to long for a garden. How he missed his and Elizabeth's garden. He took long drives through the suburbs, searching for suitable acreage he could afford. He went further out of the city where there was plenty of land for sale, but the developers had bulldozed every tree. It would take years to replace them.

Traveling back to the city, he turned onto a side road and saw a large sign, "Atholl Gardens." Curious, he turned into the parking lot and walked towards a small house which was being used as an information center. The woman inside had a broad Scottish accent. She told him that twenty acres had been donated by a philanthropist to the council, with the understanding that none of the land was to be sold to developers, and a garden to rival the Botanic Gardens was envisioned. The Board of Trustees had hired her husband, Andrew Gillespie, who had been Head Gardener at one of the great estates in the U.K. He was to design and oversee what would be an ambitious project.

"It'll take four years before the public will see the results. But why don't you go and meet my husband, he can show you around."

Timothy was astonished at what had already been accomplished. Broad winding brick paths led past enormous borders and he could see in the distance that a summerhouse with trellised sides had been erected. Timothy felt Elizabeth's presence beside him. He strolled around with Andrew, who explained what plans he had in mind for future projects.

"You're very knowledgeable Commissioner, and I can see you're itching to get your hands into the soil."

He told Andrew of his longing to have his own garden and the difficulty in finding acreage he could afford.

"Well, until you do, why don't you practice here. I can see you've got a good eye for design. Why don't you have a go with this border? The boys will soon be finished prepping the soil. We're thinking of a mixed perennial bed. Come and have a cup of coffee. I hear my wife calling me. We can discuss this further."

When he got back to the apartment, he took all of Elizabeth's journals out; notebooks and her gardening books, feeling his excitement rising as he looked at their favorite borders.

He became so involved with the work, he canceled his date with his latest companion.

"You're what?" she expostulated. "You're digging in a garden? You live in an apartment, what garden is this? What? Atholl's garden, who's he?" She spluttered, "I think you've gone crazy. You know I'm going on a cruise. I'll be away for six weeks. I won't see you when I get back."

She was still carping when he put the phone down. He was relieved that she was the one to call off the affair.

Every weekend for the next six months he spent at Atholl Gardens, enjoying his growing friendship with the Gillespies, and the feeling of peace and satisfaction he found in the manual labor.

A few months later his real estate broker called him to tell him that his tenant wouldn't be renewing her lease.

"I can easily get another good tenant, but," he hesitated, "I don't want you to think I'm pressuring you when I tell you your house has become very valuable. You might want to think of selling."

"What price were you thinking of?"

He gasped when the broker told him.

"The property in your area has gone up fantastically. Very soon it will be more valuable than Hillcrest. That's because of its proximity to the city and the University. Many older people are downsizing. Younger people are buying and remodeling. The whole character of the neighborhood is changing. Have you been here lately?"

"No, not for a few years," Timothy admitted.

"Well, you'll be in for a surprise. Why don't you meet me at the house and we can discuss what you want to do."

The main street had changed beyond all recognition. Boutiques, cafes, coffee shops, restaurants with outdoor dining under striped awnings and umbrellas. How clever Elizabeth had been to foresee all this.

A greater surprise was the change in his neighborhood. Almost all the houses had been remodeled, some with pop up roofs and small courtyards. Daniel had told him that his mother had sold their house and when she died a year later, he and his sister had inherited a tidy sum.

His broker was waiting outside his house.

"If you decide to sell, you would get a higher price because you're on a corner. Several people have already made inquiries. There might be a bidding war."

He told the broker to go ahead with the sale.

He wandered around to the cul-de-sac where he'd first met Elizabeth. Her face turned up to him, "Why, you're a Police Officer." He recalled with clarity looking into those eyes knowing he had fallen hopelessly in love, a love so intense it would forever change his life. "Oh Elizabeth," he thought, "I had you for so short a time."

Sadly he went back to his car. When he came to the four-way stop, on an impulse he decided to pass their house. He parked and walked up and down the sidewalk noting that the border where he'd spent so much time weeding was still spectacular. The garage door opened and the husband and wife came out.

"Oh are you admiring our garden?" she said.

"Yes," he replied. "It's beautiful."

"It was designed by Elizabeth Murray. Many garden clubs visit it every summer. Would you like to see the back garden?"

He felt emotional looking at the terrace where they'd entertained. He could almost feel Elizabeth's presence. The blue and white border, his gift to her, was magnificent, the only addition a small fountain burbling in the middle of the bed. They strolled past the long border. "Isn't that a stunning rose," said the owner. "It's called 'Peace.'"

"Yes, I know," he said. "It's a perfect name."

"Who was that?" asked the husband. "Did you ask his name?"

"You know, I forgot. We were so engrossed in gardening talk. But he seems to be a knowledgeable gardener."

Chapter Twenty Seven

Timothy - An Exceptional Man

Elizabeth was sitting on a bench in the courtyard of her London townhouse. A large envelope containing cuttings from the Hamilton City's newspapers sent to her by Alan was on her lap.

David had taken the children to the private park across the road. He knew she would want to read whatever was in the envelope without any distractions. She thought fondly how thoughtful he was, and what a devoted father he was, spending as much time as was possible with the children. He'd even canceled an overseas trip to stay with his adored son, who'd had a slight cold.

She poured a second cup of tea and opened the envelope. Unfolding the first cutting she gasped at the large photo of Timothy above which was a banner headline.

"COMMISSIONER DEFUSES DANGEROUS SITUATION:

Commissioner Timothy Bennet was in his office when he was informed that gang warfare had broken out between the Green Dragons and the Red Devils. It had started with members of the gang trading insults, then violence had erupted and several men had been wounded. Commissioner Bennet was driven to the chaotic scene by one of his deputies. Unarmed and accompanied only by his deputy using a bull horn, he walked into a situation fraught with danger. The deputy called on the leaders to drop their weapons and to come outside to talk to the Commissioner. Sporadic gunfire could be heard, but he stood calmly on the sidewalk waiting for the leaders to respond.

Five minutes later, they emerged and the three of them spoke for ten minutes. An hour later the gangs dispersed, averting what could have become a bloodbath and an escalation in gang violence.

At a press conference the Commissioner was questioned about the conversation with the gang leaders, Kwame Jackson and Emilio Ramirez.

'I said, you are both natural leaders, but you are leading your followers into a life of crime, long prison terms and perhaps death. You're wasting lives that could be useful to your communities. I've invited Mr. Jackson and Mr. Ramirez to a meeting in my office, where I hope we can broker a reconciliation. They've agreed and we're to meet in the morning.'"

The next cutting showed a photo of Timothy shaking hands with the two leaders. Standing on the steps in front of the Law Enforcement and Justice building, he answered the questions of the assembled press.

"These two men, Kwame Jackson and Emilio Ramirez, have shown an enormous capacity for leadership. Their decision to bring about a ceasefire will benefit both their communities. I've promised them that a small abandoned school will be renovated and that extra classrooms will be added. These two men will encourage their followers to enroll in the school where they will be taught the skills necessary for them to embark on successful careers. Mr. Jackson and Mr. Ramirez have accepted my invitation to attend a groundbreaking ceremony for the new classrooms. Ministers, pastors, community leaders will also be in attendance, as well as members of the public."

Several days later an editorial detailing the recent events ended with a paragraph praising Timothy.

"The cessation of hostilities between these two factions will lead to a decrease in gang activity, making their communities safer. Commissioner Bennet's future plans to add more trained and empathetic officers into these areas will strengthen the ties between law enforcement and the communities most affected by crime. The city owes this courageous man, Commissioner Timothy Bennet, a debt of gratitude for his bold actions and initiatives."

"Oh Timothy, sweet Timothy," Elizabeth murmured as she folded the cuttings.

David came into the courtyard.

"I see you've made Shepherd's Pie for the children's supper. Mrs. Jenkins is dishing out for them now. All that running around has given them an appetite. That pie looked so good. I wouldn't mind having some for my supper."

"No," she laughed, "I'm making you your favorite steak and roast potatoes."

She held out her hands, "Come and sit with me." She moved to give him room on the bench.

"But darling, Elizabeth, I see tears on your lovely cheeks. Not bad news?" he asked anxiously.

"No, wonderful news dearest. Here, read about Timothy. My tears are tears of joy."

When he'd finished reading he put his arm around her. "It's what I would have expected from him, he's a brave man and a great leader. He'll climb to even greater heights."

"And that's thanks to you for saving his career. You saved both of us. When I think of how your plan might have failed," she shuddered, "Timothy and I would have been destroyed by the publicity."

"Elizabeth, do you think we should write to him and..."

"No," she said firmly. "It might...no, I'll tell Alan to write and send our best wishes. Also how proud we all are of him."

He sighed, knowing that her and Timothy's love would never erode. He accepted this, and was well-aware she would never love him the way she loved Timothy. But he had been the beneficiary of the calamity which had led to their parting.

He held her closely. To wake up every morning and see this lovely creature beside him, to hear the voices of his children in the corridor outside their bedroom, wasn't this his dream come true?

Chapter Twenty Eight

A New Garden Of Eden

Mrs. Johnson buzzed him.

"Commissioner, there's a Kwame Jackson who wants to see you. Should I tell him to make an appointment for next week?"

"No, no," Timothy said. "Tell him to come right up."

"Kwame, it's great to see you, come and sit down."

Timothy ushered him into his office.

"How have you been getting on?"

"Commissioner, I've been helping out at the school, some athletic coaching, a few odd jobs here and there, but I don't feel satisfaction. I want to do something to help my community, so I've decided to join law enforcement."

"Kwame, this is great news," Timothy said with a delighted smile.

"If there's anything I can do to help you, let me know. You'll have to undergo rigorous training. That should be easy enough for you. However, what I advise is for you to do a two-year college course studying sociology and criminal justice. With a degree, it'll put you on a fast track with quicker promotions."

"Thank you Commissioner, you've told me everything I wanted to know."

Coming out of his office he said to Mrs. Johnson, "Mrs. Johnson, this is Kwame Jackson. He never has to make an appointment to see me. My door is open to him at all times."

He took Kwame down to the cafeteria where several officers were taking a coffee break.

They all stood up when Timothy approached them. He told them the news.

"Bro, this is great news," said Lieutenant Tyrone Taylor, shaking Kwame's hand.

The others also congratulated him on his decision.

When Timothy returned to his office, Mrs. Johnson said, "Andrew Gillespie called. He said it's urgent."

"Andrew, anything wrong?"

Andrew, normally composed, sounded excited.

He told Timothy of a parcel of land adjoining a horse farm which would soon be coming on the market. It was an estate sale, and the heirs were keen sellers.

"Timothy, if you put in an offer now it would be a clean sale, no commission on either side. You could get it for a song, because the garden needs a lot of work and the caretaker's cottage is in a sorry condition. Timothy, this is one of the nicest pieces of land I've seen. After work, come here and I'll take you to see it. It's near to Atholl Gardens."

"But where is it?" Timothy felt his interest quickening.

"Glendower Estates."

"But that's the most expensive area in Hamilton City, I don't think I could afford to..."

"Believe me," said Andrew earnestly, "this property is going for a song. You won't regret it, but be quick and put in a low offer."

As soon as he walked through the rickety gates, Timothy knew he'd found his ideal acreage. Mature trees, large shrubs which would need pruning, and as Andrew pointed out, many existing beds now overgrown with weeds.

"The wife of the caretaker started this garden twenty years ago. It shouldn't take long to clean it up."

The cottage was in bad condition, but with a few changes and upgrades it could be made habitable. There was a large kitchen, two bedrooms and two bathrooms, a small dining room and a nice sized living room.

"The first thing I'd do is knock out the wall between the dining room and living room. Make it one big room where I could build bookshelves. Eventually I want a terrace stretching the length of the house. Otherwise, for the time being, no other changes."

Andrew showed him the two stables not far from the cottage.

"One day these could be converted into a guest suite, connected to the cottage with a courtyard," Timothy said.

"A million ideas, my friend, and all of them good. I think you'll be kept busy for the next thirty years," Andrew said.

That night he slept very little. His mind was filled with plans.

Oh Elizabeth, my love, my teacher and advisor. Though you won't be physically with me, I know you'll be with me in spirit, guiding me as I create our new Garden of Eden. He finally fell asleep in the early hours; gardening books, journals and notebooks spread out around him on the bed.

The sale went through without difficulty. The low price left him with a still-healthy bank balance, enough to create the garden he had longed for.

Two months later Timothy and Andrew sat in the renovated kitchen.

"I must say I like this kitchen," Andrew said as he and Timothy sat at Elizabeth's table, sipping tea and sampling the scones sent by his wife. "You've done an excellent job with very little expense and renovation."

The old stone floor had been scraped, sanded and varnished. New appliances and a sink installed. The small laundry room now boasted a recently purchased washer and dryer.

"You know," continued Andrew, "these old houses were really well built. They're solid, not like the flimsy structures being built today. But let's take a stroll around and you can tell me what designs you have in mind. I like the idea of a sunken garden with wide steps leading down to it. It's ambitious but doable. It would really divide the garden into separate areas. I think you're aiming for an authentic English style? And those trees on the property line, are you thinking of taking any out?"

"No," said Timothy. How he enjoyed discussing his plans with Andrew, and how eternally grateful he would be to him for his advice and incomparable help. It must have been a benevolent fate that had led him onto that side road.

"I was thinking of a woodland garden with a flagstone path winding through the trees which would link up with the area leading to the rose garden. The woodland area to be planted with columbine, bleeding heart, hosta, ferns, maybe azaleas and hydrangeas."

The following week Andrew visited again with an interesting proposal. "I had a meeting with the board members. They've suggested that with the garden taking shape, within two or three years it would be ready to be opened to the public. Because you'll need heavy equipment to reshape certain areas, they'd be willing to rent out the equipment at a nominal price and also to provide the necessary labor you'd need in maintaining these large borders. In return you'd allow them to have groups of garden clubs and other members of the public to tour. The money raised would benefit Atholl Gardens. What do you think?"

Timothy readily accepted this generous proposal.

Daniel was arriving for a weeklong visit. A maid had prepared the small bedroom, furnished with pieces from Elizabeth's collection.

"Well," said Daniel as they inspected what was to become a garden. "Quite frankly, Commissioner, this all looks like crap to me, and what are you going to do with these old sheds?"

Timothy laughed, "Your trouble, Daniel, is that you have no imagination. Wait until you come back next year. The sheds, as you so kindly put it, will soon be converted into a guest suite for you. You can invite friends, or," he smiled, "a companion. I want you to think of this place as your home."

Within three years Timothy's dream was a reality with garden clubs booking well in advance. They were eager to see this garden which was generating much publicity and enthusiasm in the local press.

In the summer months, Timothy rose at dawn so that he could get in a few hours of digging and weeding before going to work. In the evening he worked until dark, and after dinner fell into bed exhausted. On the weekends he worked non-stop. He had never felt so fit. There was no need to go to the gym, every muscle in his body felt fine tuned. In the heat of the day with his shirt off, he acquired an enviable tan. He thought of Elizabeth warning him about taking his shirt off, a beautiful woman in a convertible might pass and kidnap him. Reminiscing, he sighed, thinking that there was no Elizabeth to come out brandishing a frying pan to come and rescue him.

The only tree planted was "Autumn Purple Ash," the tree against which Elizabeth had been silhouetted that memorable day when she'd said she'd marry him. He planted it outside his bedroom, where through the window he could view it as he sat in her rocking chair.

He made a start on the area which was to be a replica of the blue and white bed he'd designed for Elizabeth. But this area was four times the size and was overrun with weeds. On a Saturday morning, Andrew found Timothy in despair at the work involved in ridding the enormous area of weeds.

"This looks like more than a month of hard labor," Andrew said. "These weeds are a bugger, the gardener's enemy. They're entrenched. It'll be impossible to plant anything until every root is eradicated. Timothy, I'll send two chaps with a mechanical deep digger, also a sieve. The whole area has to be sieved to make sure that no roots remain. In two weeks once the soil has been amended, you should be able to start planting. Will you need help with the planting?"

"No thanks, Andrew, I want to do it all myself."

"Tell me what you have in mind."

Timothy described the vision he had.

"Blue and white with two paths leading up to a gazebo?"

Andrew said, "No doubt you've been inspired by the white garden at Sissinghurst? But this sounds even more interesting, adding the blue to the mix. 'Sally Holmes' creeping up the gazebo and six 'Iceberg' roses in the center flanked by blue delphiniums sounds stunning. Timothy, if you can pull this off it'll make this garden famous not only in Hamilton City but in the state."

***

The house was filled with Elizabeth's furniture, which he'd taken out of storage. In the library section of the enlarged room, the bookshelves were stacked and arranged as she had done; fiction and non-fiction. As he looked around his small house, he felt a measure of happiness surrounded by her belongings and all the memories they evoked.

Daniel was flying in for the long weekend.

"Timothy, do you mind if I ask a few friends to come on Saturday night? I thought we could have a barbecue. I'll help you. I'll get all the salads at the deli, and set the table."

Timothy, who was between companions, was happy to meet Daniel's friends. Though he was concerned that Daniel was sliding into a relationship with his girlfriend, Shelley, whom he'd met on a few occasions. Several times she had flown to Washington, D.C. to visit Daniel—visits, Timothy felt, that were being used to cement their relationship. Shelley was too clinging, constantly touching Daniel, rubbing his neck, and murmuring intimately into his ear.

"Daniel you must be careful that you don't become too entangled with Shelley," he warned. "She seems a nice girl, but you mustn't confuse sex with love. It's a common mistake, and by the way, are you using protection? I've seen many young lives ruined by being careless in this regard."

Daniel laughed. "Don't worry, Timothy, I am careful."

"Well, I'm just telling you this because you might find it difficult to break with her without a lot of trauma."

Timothy had ambitious plans for Daniel. He was good-looking, with an engaging personality, and he would have a brilliant career ahead of him. To be tethered to a not very bright girl with an irritating giggle was not a thought that comforted him. Besides, she was four years older than Daniel, far too experienced for him.

"I've asked my former football coach from high school, as well as Shelley's friend. She's recently divorced. I'm sure you'll like her. Her name's Courtney."

Timothy sighed, Daniel was matchmaking again.

It was a perfect evening for a barbecue. The talk was lively, the former coach had a fund of stories that kept them laughing.

The divorced friend, Courtney, bore a superficial likeness to Elizabeth; a pretty smile, which he noted, never seemed to reach her eyes, which were shrewd and calculating. He and the coach shared an interest in ancient history. They were discussing Paris' kidnapping of Helen of Troy when Courtney interrupted.

"Paris? Oh I'm dying to visit Paris. All that fabulous shopping. I want to, like, plan a trip for next year."

Timothy's slight interest in her waned.

Before it became dark, they went for a stroll in the garden, stopping in front of the blue and white border. Bending down Timothy broke off some sprigs of lavender and gallantly presented them to the girls.

Courtney wrinkled her nose, then sneezed twice.

"I don't like this smell. I'm like allergic to flowers."

He looked at her feet in their dainty sandals. Ugh! Flat, broad, and with fat toes and calluses on her heels. Whatever interest he might have had in her disappeared completely.

Walking back to the house, she took his arm and said, "So will you think of renovating the house? If you decide to I've got a friend who's a divine interior decorator. You must let me introduce you."

He stared at her. "It has been renovated. I don't intend to do any more."

She was disappointed when he ushered her to her car. She'd been hoping for an invitation to sleep over.

"I'm having a party next week, will you come?"

"Er, um," he stammered. "I'll be out of town, but," not wanting to hurt her feelings, he smiled warmly, "some other time."

218

Driving home she was pleased with the way the evening had turned out. He had been eyeing her breasts all evening. She had no doubt that she could capture him, but he'd have to sell that house, and get rid of that old boring furniture. As for that garden, to her way of thinking as she'd viewed the vast stretches of grass, it looked like a mowing headache. She'd get him to buy one of those mansions she'd seen on her drive into the suburbs and of course some decent modern furniture.

"Well," said Daniel eagerly, "what did you think of her?"

"Daniel," said Timothy sternly. "Please, no more matchmaking."

Lying in bed that night, Timothy was grateful that no callused feet would be scraping against his legs.

Chapter Twenty Nine

An Enduring Love

After the Chief Commissioner retired, Timothy was appointed Chief. He was the youngest man ever to hold that position. In a large room in a downtown hotel, he and three of his officers were still sitting around the oval table where a successful conference had just concluded. Law enforcement officials from several states had been in attendance, the main topic on the agenda being the increase in gang activity in two of the states, and how to deal with a new menace, more powerful drugs coming onto the market.

Timothy said, "Well, that went well, I was proud of the way you guys handled some difficult questions, and I could see that some of the proposals you put forward impressed everyone."

He stood up. "I'll meet you in the restaurant. Go ahead and order, and if they've got shrimp I'll have it as an appetizer. I want to stretch my legs."

He walked up the stairs to the mezzanine level and leaning on the railing looked down into the foyer. He was relieved that the conference was over. Dealing with all those egos had been a strain. He'd had to use patience and diplomacy to avert any discord that could have developed. Now he could relax and enjoy an evening with his boys. A jolt like electricity went through him. Elizabeth was coming into the foyer with David and two children. His hands gripped the railing. He had to restrain himself from calling down to her.

David and the children went into a side room. She spoke briefly to the receptionist at the front desk, smiled, and then she walked to the elevator.

He raced down the stairs, but the elevator doors had already closed.

He said to the receptionist, "I've just seen Lady Elizabeth Knightley going up to her suite. I'd like to call her."

She gave him the suite number. The phone rang six times before she answered.

He found it difficult to speak.

"Elizabeth. It's Timothy."

"Timothy? Is that really you? Where are you?"

"In the foyer, Elizabeth, I must see you."

She hesitated. "But we're leaving in an hour. David is saying goodbye to some friends..."

"Elizabeth, please I'm begging you. I must see you."

"Alright, where should we meet?"

"There's a coffee shop just off the foyer. I'll wait for you there."

Waiting for her he felt as nervous as on the day he'd first met her in that cul-de-sac. He sat on a bench outside the coffee shop, which was being remodeled. He could see the workmen packing up to leave. There was no traffic here. The elevator doors opened and he was dumbstruck at how little she had changed. She was still so beautiful. Her smile when she saw him radiant, her eyes luminous as she looked at him.

He stood up and took her hands kissing them.

"Elizabeth," he murmured. "I can't believe I'm actually looking at you."

"Timothy, let's sit down. My legs feel a bit shaky."

"You've cut your hair," he said accusingly.

"Yes, it was too long, and I didn't want to look like mutton dressed as lamb."

"Mutton? What do you mean?"

"Well, you know when women grow older, they try to look young by dressing inappropriately. And of course they're not fooling anyone, so to avoid that fate I cut my hair."

He burst out laughing. "Oh God, I've not been with you two minutes and you're making me laugh."

They sat gazing at each other, the longing in his eyes mirrored in her own.

He caressed her hands. "Elizabeth, are you happy?"

"Yes I am, not of course as happy as I was with you, that could never be possible. But David has been so good to me; he adores me, and caters to my every whim." She smiled. "I hope I don't have too many of those. Also I have two wonderful children, and a peaceful, protected life, but my sweet Timothy, I've never stopped loving you or longing for you."

He was so moved by her declaration he found it difficult to speak.

"Elizabeth, I have to hold you."

She moved away, alarmed.

"No Timothy, not in public."

"There's no traffic here because of the remodeling. The workmen have gone, and that alcove they were working on, let's go in there. Nobody will see us."

In the alcove they stood locked in each other's arms. They were overcome by the force of their emotions. His hands under her jacket felt again her silken skin, the curve of her spine, knowing every contour of the body he had worshiped.

"Elizabeth, I can feel your ribs, are you losing weight?"

"I have a bit. It's all this running around. David can't bear to be parted from me or the children, so I've been on several trips with him, but this will be my last. I'm much happier at home."

"Yes," he said. "You always were happier at home, waiting for me to come off my shifts, cooking for me, spoiling me."

He held her even closer. "Oh God, I feel I'm dreaming, holding you, wanting you, if only we could..."

"No Timothy, what you're thinking of is impossible. I would never be disloyal to David, even standing here with you makes me feel guilty."

"I'm looking forward to Daniel's visit to the U.K. next month. He writes to me often, keeping me informed of all your triumphs, your garden, of course, and your hectic social life."

She caressed his neck, then his face and with her forefinger gently traced around his mouth. He felt chills going up and down his spine.

He half sang, half whispered.
"You left me for another's arms,
Now he owns your many charms,
Your kisses that once were mine,
Your soft embraces so divine.
I see you when I close my eyes
Hear your voice, your tender sighs."

"Timothy stop." She leaned away from him. "I can't bear to hear that music, those words. I never listen to that old music anymore. It makes me feel sad. I'll treasure this meeting as long as I live but Timothy," she said urgently, "there's something I must tell you..." She paused. "It's important."

"What my darling? Tell me."

She hesitated. "No, there isn't enough time, it's too complicated. I must go. Hand me my purse."

He retrieved it from the floor.

She took out a lipstick and applied it to her lips.

"But I always preferred your mouth without lipstick."

"I know, but David would notice. Oh darn, I don't have a tissue in this purse."

"Here," he took out his handkerchief and she blotted her lips.

He folded the handkerchief carefully before putting it in his pocket.

"And now," her lips trembled, "it's goodbye. Remember, my sweet Timothy, I will always love you. When I draw my last breath my thoughts will be of you."

"Oh Elizabeth," he groaned. "My life, no matter how successful, is empty without you."

He watched as she walked swiftly away. Trying to control his emotions, he sat down on the bench, putting his head in his hands. He could smell her lavender perfume on them. He took out his handkerchief and gazed at the imprint of her lips, then he folded it and put in an inner pocket.

Eventually, feeling calmer, he joined his officers in the restaurant.

"Hope you don't mind Chief, we were starving. So we started eating. The food here is great. We ordered the shrimp for you."

"Go ahead you guys, and order whatever you want."

He looked at the shrimp. He'd lost his appetite. His hands were still shaking slightly as he broke a roll in half and buttered it. The half hour spent with Elizabeth was seared into his memory.

***

Two months later, Washington D.C.
Daniel's letter.

"Dear Chief,

It was great seeing you last month. I really liked the girl you introduced me to. I hope to see her again on my next visit to you. But didn't you say no more matchmaking???

First of all, I want to thank you for arranging this trip to the U.K., it was fantastic. I stayed for several days with Alan. He hasn't changed. He's still a great guy. Then I visited your friend (Sir David's cousin) at London Law Enforcement. He wants you to know he's very impressed with your initiatives for curbing gang violence, and he'll contact you when he visits the States next year. And now to the most important part of my trip, and which I know you're anxious to hear about, my meeting with Elizabeth.

I spoke to Sir David and he said she was very excited about seeing me, unfortunately though she was recovering from, did he say flu or pneumonia? I would only be able to see her for an hour or so. He invited me for tea at 4:00p.m. I arrived at the townhouse. What a beautiful area, lots of trees and a small park opposite it. The door was opened by a guy in a smart dark suit. I thought he must be a relative, an uncle maybe, but thank goodness I didn't try to shake his hand. It turned out he was the butler. The entrance hall was quite narrow, and was tiled in black and white marble. He opened double doors and I went into the most beautiful room I'd ever seen or will ever see again. High ceilings, paneled walls and four huge arched windows. Chief, to give you an idea of how big this room was, there were three seating areas, a grand piano in one corner and paintings lining one wall, people in wigs and old fashioned clothes, Sir David's ancestors I guess. The last painting was of Elizabeth and the children. I can't describe how magnificent she looked. I couldn't take my eyes off it.

And then I turned and saw her. She was smiling. Oh those dimples. She must have been watching me as I toured the room. She was lying on a sort of couch, propped up with cushions and a blue blanket covered her.

She held out her hands. 'Daniel, my darling Daniel, what a tonic it is to see you.'

I didn't know whether I should kiss her, but she took my hands and kissed them. Chief you can imagine how touched I felt when she did that.

'Pull up that chair,' she said, 'so that I can really feast my eyes on you, you're even more handsome than when I last saw you, my darling rescuer.'

A few minutes later the butler guy came in with a tray which he put on a table, he asked if he should pour the tea.

'No thank you,' she said, 'my friend will pour. Daniel, you still remember how to pour tea?'

And what a tea. It reminded me of the tea parties on your terrace, little cucumber sandwiches, scones and a plate of delicious small pastries filled with, I don't know what it was. She ate only one sandwich and half a scone, but I'm ashamed to say I made a pig of myself.

She laughed at me. 'Oh Daniel, you've still got a good appetite. I always enjoyed cooking for you.'

She seemed a bit tired. 'Darling, could you put another cushion behind me, I seem to be sliding down. And tuck that blanket around my legs more firmly, my feet feel so cold.'

As I lifted her foot, I remembered the first time we met in that cul-de-sac. You held her foot. Do you remember Chief? She looked so fragile lying there and so helpless. It made me sad, she'd always been the strong one, always dashing about, helping everyone. She must have had a bad bout of the flu.

'Daniel, I'll nap for a few minutes, why don't you go into the courtyard, I want you to describe it to Timothy.'

An amazing courtyard, narrow but very long, high brick walls, stuff growing on them (I don't know the names of any plants). Against the far wall a fantastic fountain, three sinks splashing into a pond. There were two huge containers filled with plants.

When I went back inside she was awake. She again took my hands and said, 'Daniel, I want you to give Timothy a message. Tell him I often think of him, and give him my very best love.'

She looked quite agitated. 'You won't forget?'

I promised her.

She sighed and said, 'What fun we used to have. I'll never forget those happy days in Hamilton City.'

Once again she seemed to tire.

'Daniel, I hear Sir David and the children in the hall,' she pressed my hands and said urgently, 'you won't forget to give Timothy my message?'

I said I wouldn't forget. I told her as soon as I got back home I'd tell you.

'Sir David will want to sit next to me. Why don't you move to the opposite chair?'

Sir David and the children came in. What a wonderful man. He welcomed me and said, 'I can see your visit has cheered Elizabeth.'

He sat on the chair next to her and took her hand. Their son Hugh—what a handsome boy—sat on the couch and held her other hand, while the little girl (the image of her mother), stood next to Sir David, her hand on his shoulder.

They never took their eyes off Elizabeth. I felt I was in the way, so I said goodbye, and hoped she'd soon be well.

'I hope you'll excuse my not seeing you to the door, Daniel,' Sir David said. 'Hugh will see you out.'

Hugh stood on the sidewalk with me until the cab came. He shook my hand. 'It was a pleasure meeting you, sir. Mother often talks about you.'

What a good-looking kid. He reminded me of someone. I couldn't think who, maybe a photo I'd seen in a magazine, or perhaps in a movie.

So that was my visit to Elizabeth. I hope that it all made sense to you.

Love,

Daniel

P.S. Next to her on a small table were all the magazines I'd sent her, where your garden was featured. The top one was the blue and white garden which was on the cover of *Influential Gardens*.

Her message to you again.

'Tell Timothy I often think of him, and give him my very best love.'"

Chapter Thirty

Gone But Not Forgotten

Saturday was Timothy's favorite day of the week. As an early riser, he went out into the garden as soon as it was light, checking the borders for weeds, hoeing, dividing perennials that were outgrowing their spaces and inspecting the roses for signs of diseases.

After two hours, he sat with a cup of coffee in the summerhouse which overlooked the main rose garden. The six "Peace" roses were full of buds, some starting to open. They would elicit many oohs and aahs from the garden club members. Andrew and his helpers would be coming in the afternoon to mow the lawns and generally tidy up. The week ahead would be busy with the beginning of the tour season. Four tours were booked at the end of the week and one club was coming from out of state. Andrew and his wife would be their guides. On Saturday and Sunday he would take over, giving advice and answering questions.

He opened the morning newspaper. On the front page was a photo of Elizabeth! Under the obituary headline it said:

"Lady Elizabeth Knightley died two days ago in her London townhouse. Lady Knightley was on the Board of the Hamilton City Botanic Gardens for many years. A talented designer and writer, she was also a strong supporter of law enforcement, raising over $200,000 for the Police Fund. She is survived by her husband, Sir David Knightley, and her three children. A memorial remembrance will be held at the Botanic Gardens on Monday at 11:00a.m."

He sat stunned, unable to move. How was this possible?

Eventually, tears streaming down his cheeks, he walked unsteadily into the house to call Daniel.

"No," sobbed Daniel. "She was recovering from the flu. I sat holding her hands. She never complained or hinted that anything was wrong. Timothy, I can't speak to you now. I'm too overcome. Our darling, Elizabeth. We both loved her so much. I'll call you later."

Yes, that was his Elizabeth. So brave, so uncomplaining, never wanting to cause worry to anyone. How could he live in a world without her?

He spoke to Daniel again, then switched his calls to the answering machine. He called the hostess of the dinner party he was to attend that evening. He was relieved that he could leave a message on her answering machine. He apologized for canceling at the last minute. He was in no state to be making lighthearted conversations at a dinner party.

When Andrew arrived with the boys, he could see that something had happened to his friend. When Timothy told him without going into the details that a dear friend had died, he put his arm around Timothy's shoulder, trying to comfort him.

"Timothy, can we help in any way?"

"No, thank you. I'm just grateful to have you as my friend. What would I do without you? I know you'll see to everything for the tours."

For the memorial service he wore the uniform she admired at their meeting in the hotel.

"You look so handsome," she'd murmured. "It's not fair. You're getting better-looking as you get older. Who could resist you?"

He arrived early at the Botanic Gardens, knowing that crowds would soon fill the reception hall. A dozen people were standing at the far end of the hall, looking at three photos on easels. The central photo had been enlarged. He gasped at how lifelike it was. She was wearing a strapless dress, her hair swept up on top of her head. He remembered that dress, and the benefit too. He had been distraught watching her and the men clamoring to dance with her.

A smaller photo on the left hand side showed her with her children. They were dressed in white, probably a garden party, he thought. He could see borders of flowers in the background. The photo on the right hand side was of her and David, dressed for some sort of gala. Her black dress was low cut, revealing her shoulders and the tops of her breasts gleaming under the lights. He felt his throat constrict as he looked at David who was half-turned towards her, his arm around her possessively. He gazed, mesmerized at the central photo—how alive she looked, her eyes seemed to be staring into his, her joyful smile.

Over the P.A. system floated the rich voice of Nat King Cole singing "Unforgettable"—one of their favorite songs.

The words made his heart ache.

He found it unbearable listening to that music and the memories it evoked. He turned and made his way through the crowd. Coming in at the main door he saw Commander Juan Sanchez and six officers from his precinct. It would be impossible to speak to them. He wouldn't be able to control his emotions. He went through a side door and into the area leading to the parking lot. The music following him.

A huge crowd was waiting to enter the reception hall.

He could see more cruisers and squad cars arriving.

He thought, Elizabeth, you were wrong. You haven't been forgotten by the people whose lives you touched. You will be remembered for your grace, your beauty and the exemplary life you led. My sweet Elizabeth, you are unforgettable.

Just before he reached the parking lot, he passed a bed of English lavender—her perfume. He stopped and broke off a sprig. Walking to his car, he could feel Elizabeth's presence beside him.

"Timothy, I've told you lavender will wilt and die unless you put it immediately into water. That sprig will be dead by the time you get to your office."

And it was dead, as dead as Elizabeth.

Before going up to his office, he sat in his car, choked with tears as he pictured her in the coffin, her eyes closed forever, that smile that had so entranced him, gone, all gone.

"Elizabeth, you've left us at the peak of your beauty. That's how you'll be remembered."

***

Weeks later as Timothy was about to leave his office, Mrs. Johnson came in with a package.

"This has just been delivered, Chief. Should I leave it on your desk?"

"Thank you Mrs. Johnson, I'll open it in the car."

Smaller than a shoebox, it was wrapped in brown paper and secured with tape. It was postmarked San Diego.

Once in the car, he tore off the paper and a wooden box with painted flowers was revealed. He opened the brass clasp and lifted the lid. With trembling fingers he opened the envelope marked "Timothy." It was Elizabeth's handwriting:

"My dearest sweetest Timothy,

I've entrusted this box to my sister Mary who will be in the U.S. later this month. I didn't want to ask David to mail it. It would have hurt him to know I was writing to you at this last stage of my life. He is such a good man, and my dearest friend and advisor.

I'm returning the Jane Austen book you gave me on our last night together. How often over the years I've held it and kissed your signature.

The small parcel in tissue paper is my engagement ring. The ring I wore with such pride. Timothy, I am confident you'll meet someone who'll love you and take care of you, someone who'll be worthy of you. My darling, you can't continue to live alone, drifting from one affair to another. When you find this girl or woman, grasp this chance of happiness with both hands. Give her my ring. Together with my blessing."

Two days later the letter continued:

"I want to add this to my letter:

In my will I have left you a bequest of $100,000. This is to make sure you'll have enough money to maintain your garden. To Daniel I'm leaving $50,000. That darling boy who brought us together in that cul-de-sac. I can still remember when I looked at your face and knew I'd found my ideal man, the love of my life. What joy and passion you gave me.

Also, I'm leaving $20,000 to the school you founded, the Timothy Bennet School for Academic Achievement. The remainder of my estate will be divided equally among my children. I consulted David about these bequests and he is in complete agreement with my decisions.

They'll be here soon to move me. David will be coming in. Mary is sitting next to me. I'll give her the box.

With my last breath, my thoughts will be of you.
Yours forever,
E…"

She hadn't been able to complete her name.

Also, there was a photo of her and her son, Hugh. He stared at it puzzled. Why not a photo of her daughter as well? The boy didn't look like David and although he had his mother's blue eyes, the shape was different. His features too were different. Elizabeth and David had slightly curly hair, this boy's hair was darker and straight. Good God, was it possible that this boy was his and Elizabeth's son? Their last night together?

She had wanted to tell him something the last time he'd met her in the hotel, her voice had been urgent.

"I have to tell you something, but no," she'd said, "there isn't enough time."

He knew he would never be able to reveal this secret. Elizabeth would not have wanted him to disturb the tranquility of his son's life, or for that matter, David's.

But his and Elizabeth's love would live on in this boy.

He looked again at the photo, "My boy," he murmured, "Hugh, our son."

[Gentle Reader: You will have to decide whether there is any factual evidence to support Timothy's belief that Hugh was his son. Was it wishful thinking on his part? What was it that Elizabeth had wanted to tell him that day in the hotel. That she was ill? Perhaps she regretted leaving him? Or that Hugh was his son? You, the reader, can speculate and arrive at your own conclusion.]

Chapter Thirty One

Victoria

A month before he had met Elizabeth at the hotel, Timothy had been having an affair with a woman who was attractive and discreet. She had, however, an unappealing habit which drove him to distraction. Whenever he told her an amusing story (she had a good sense of humor), she would throw her head back and with her mouth wide open, would emit a sound—something between a honk or a bark—revealing at the back of her throat a waggling uvula. It was an unnerving sight, so to avoid a repeat of this performance he had had to scale back his fund of anecdotes.

Another irritant was her dog; a miniature dachshund, a breed he detested. She insisted that he had to lie on a cushion on the floor (the dog, not Timothy) and at crucial moments the hound would start yapping, or even worse, howling, disturbing Timothy's concentration, and even on one memorable occasion rendering him incapable of completing his lovemaking. He was relieved, therefore, when she announced that her husband had been transferred and that sadly their affair was at an end. She joined her husband in the great state of Texas, taking with her her yapping dog, her honking/barking laugh and her waggling uvula.

That was to be his last affair, because after his meeting with Elizabeth at the hotel, and shortly after her death, he entered a period of such mourning and heartache, he lost all interest in any new conquests.

[Gentle Reader: Elizabeth had been confident that Timothy would meet someone who would love and care for him. This happened when he met the girl who was to become his wife. Her name was Victoria.]

Timothy usually went into his office through his private entrance. He rarely went into the main office, leaving it in the capable hands of Mrs. Johnson. This day though he'd been visiting an officer on the second floor, and rather than going through the passage leading to his private entrance, he pushed open the door to the main office. He greeted Mrs. Johnson then noticed a new employee sitting at a desk next to her. She looked up briefly, half-smiled, then lowered her eyes to the work she was doing.

Pale complexion, he noted, almost like, what was the word? Alabaster. The only color in her face was a faint pink lipstick. Her dark glossy hair pulled back into a loose bun at the nape of her neck. But it was her eyes that caught his attention, slightly slanted, more green than hazel and well defined eyebrows. Her face was a perfect oval and put him in mind of a painting of a Madonna.

When Mrs. Johnson came into his office, he said, "I see there's a new employee?"

"Yes, Chief, a wonderful girl. I wish we had another dozen like her. She's friendly without being familiar. I've never seen her gossiping or eyeing the officers like some of the other girls. An old fashioned girl, she grew up in a small town and worked in the bank there. She moved here because she wanted to take extra courses in the city, computer technology."

"What's her name?"

"Victoria Vincent. Her Italian grandfather's last name was Vincenti, but he dropped the 'I.' Her mother's Danish."

He had never known Mrs. Johnson to be so garrulous. She had obviously taken a strong liking to this girl.

"Yes," she continued. "She was engaged for two years, but she broke it off—he was an alcoholic and drug user. He's now in Alaska. She's so competent. I've put her second in charge."

The following week when he buzzed Mrs. Johnson, Victoria answered, "Yes, Chief?"

"Oh Mrs. Johnson's not there?"

"No sir, she had a dental appointment."

"Well if you're finished with those files, you can bring them in to me."

"Yes Chief. I also have the bids from two more contractors for the building of that classroom at your school. I've checked all the figures, but I think perhaps you should get a few more bids."

He stood up when she came in.

"Are you happy with your job? You seem to have settled in well."

"Thank you sir, I'm very happy."

He liked her demeanor. It was natural, no artifice or coyness. He also approved of the way she dressed, usually wearing a pleated skirt, with a high necked fitted top which flattered her slender waist and shapely hips.

The following week when she came into his office, he came round his desk and stood looking into those remarkable eyes.

"Miss Vincent, Victoria, may I call you Victoria? I'd like to take you to dinner, a night when you don't have classes to go to."

She looked startled.

"Who me?"

He laughed.

"I don't see anyone else standing with you, so it must be you I'm inviting."

He found her company restful. Her gentle disposition and obvious vulnerability roused his protective instincts. He had no doubt Elizabeth would have approved. That this was the girl she'd hoped he would meet.

"Grasp this happiness," she'd written.

Four months later he proposed to her in the summerhouse overlooking the rose bed. From his pocket he took Elizabeth's engagement ring.

"My former wife Elizabeth, a woman I loved dearly, instructed me to give this ring to you with her blessing. Victoria I love you, and I know I can make you happy."

Victoria had loved him from the first day she'd seen him talking to Mrs. Johnson. On the occasions when she'd been in his office, her innate shyness prevented her from initiating any conversation. His dinner invitation had taken her by surprise, but gradually she had relaxed, her passion for him growing with each meeting.

One day with everyone at lunch, she'd gone into the small conference room next to his office. One wall was filled with photographs of all the past Chiefs. Her eye was drawn to a photo of Timothy and a beautiful woman standing with him. She was puzzled. Who could this woman be, the only woman amongst all these men? She asked Mrs. Johnson.

"Oh," she said. "That was Elizabeth Bennet. She and the Chief were the handsomest couple in Hamilton City. He adored her. When she was in the room, he hardly took his eyes off her. It's to honor her that she's in the photo. She worked tirelessly to raise money for the Police Fund. She was so talented and so kind, I loved her dearly."

"But what happened to her?"

Mrs. Johnson sighed.

"After five years they divorced. She went to live in England. She later married Sir David Knightley."

"Was she having an..."

Mrs. Johnson interrupted her.

"An affair? Never. Mrs. Bennet was a very moral woman. It's a mystery why they parted. They were so much in love. She was a wonderful gardener. She was on the Board of the Botanic Gardens. She died recently. Thousands came to pay their respects to her at a remembrance for her at the Gardens."

Victoria became obsessed with this story and with Elizabeth Bennet. As she studied the photo she realized she was beginning to love this woman the way Mrs. Johnson and so many others had loved her.

Now in the summerhouse, she said, "I feel honored to have Elizabeth's ring on my finger. I will treasure it always. I hope I'll be able to live up to the high standards she set."

He kissed her. "Elizabeth would be pleased and she would have loved you too."

Before she could stop herself, Victoria said, "But Timothy, what happened..."

The expression on his face warned her not to probe too deeply. She knew then that the mystery of Elizabeth's departure would forever remain unsolved.

For the next ten years Timothy had an idyllic life, wrapped in the warmth of Victoria's love, watching their two children playing in the garden making plans for their future. He worked tirelessly in the garden, for it had gained national recognition as the ideal English style garden.

As Chief Commissioner he worked long hours, executing even bolder methods to combat crime and gang violence. The school he had founded continued to prosper. Many new recruits in the Police Academy came from the school.

He treasured his friendship with the Gillespies, who were often invited to enjoy Victoria's cooking, an Italian or Danish evening.

"You know Timothy," Andrew said, "I think Atholl Gardens got the better end of the deal with you. The money raised from all the tours and galas has far surpassed anything we could have envisaged."

"No Andrew," Timothy replied, "I'm the one to thank you. You've become a very dear friend. I never would have achieved all this without your help and advice. It would have been a lovely garden, but what we see today is unique."

Every Saturday morning in the spring and summer, Timothy, Victoria and the children visited the blue and white area, which had been featured on the covers of many magazines. A brass plaque had been installed in the front of the border:

"Elizabeth Bennet
An Exceptional Woman
A Great Gardener."

He had explained to Victoria, "This is my tribute to Elizabeth, and a remembrance of the first blue and white border I designed for her. She was the one who taught me and guided me on this exciting journey."

As they gazed at the beauty before them, Timothy would break off a sprig of lavender and hand it to Victoria.

"Elizabeth's perfume. Whenever you smell this, you'll be reminded of her. And now my darling Victoria, I have you and the children to complete my happiness."

***

It was in the early hours that the pain woke him. He sat up gasping. His stomach felt tender as he pressed his hands against it. He swung his legs over the side of the bed and sat waiting for the pain to subside. Ten minutes later he went into the kitchen, perhaps a glass of warm milk would help.

Twenty minutes later the pain had decreased. He went back to bed but slept fitfully.

It must have been that late dinner, he thought. I overate and that second glass of wine was a mistake.

Two weeks later the pain returned, but this time it was of a longer duration. Now he realized it wasn't indigestion. He'd eaten very little the night before. Not wanting to alarm Victoria, he called from his office to make an appointment with his doctor.

"Well, Chief," the doctor said after examining him. "We're going to run some tests."

Sitting in the doctor's office waiting to hear the results of the tests, Timothy could see that the doctor's face was grave.

"Chief, I'm sure you'd want to hear the truth. I'm afraid it's pancreatic cancer, which we can treat aggressively with surgery and chemotherapy."

Timothy's mouth had gone dry.

"How much time would that give me?"

"A year, maybe more."

"And if I do nothing?"

"Chief, it pains me to tell you, maybe six months."

So this is it, he thought grimly, driving back to his office, contemplating what lay ahead. In his office he prepared a letter of resignation. No use postponing it. His affairs would have to be wound up while he still had the strength and resolution to do so.

Two days later he called a meeting with Andrew and the board members. Explaining to the shocked members how little time he had left, he outlined a plan which he had carefully thought out. He would cede the deeds and ownership of his property to Atholl Gardens.

He said, "It will in effect become an adjunct of the Gardens. This is the only way the garden will be saved from being destroyed. Victoria will never be able to handle the complexities of running this garden. She will be financially secure. The life policy I took out when our daughter was born is very large and will ensure that she and the children will always be independent. An important stipulation is that she and the children will be allowed to stay on in the house for however long she wishes. I will die knowing that the garden is being left in good hands."

He continued, "Andrew, will you see that the lawyers draw up the papers so that my wishes and instructions are clearly understood?"

After he'd left them, Andrew and the Board members were overcome with grief.

"A brave man," they said, "a man who has lived his life with grace and dignity. There'll never be another like him."

That night after dinner, he sat with Victoria and told her the news.

"I've resigned so that I can spend as much time as possible with you and the children."

He explained the terms he had reached with Atholl Gardens.

"Your secure life won't change."

"Timothy," she wept. "How can I live without you?"

"You must be brave, my pet, for the sake of the children."

Four months later, weakened by the constant pain, he was unable to get out of bed.

The doctor spoke to Victoria.

"It's time for hospice to take over, day and night nursing. You and your mother won't be able to cope with the final stages."

Several days later, with Victoria holding his hand, he was given the final dosage of painkiller. Before it took hold, Timothy had a vision of Elizabeth sitting on his lap on the rocking chair, the glowing tree behind her. She was looking into his eyes, her smile radiant.

"Oh Timothy, I love you so. I will marry you."

As he took his last breath, he whispered,

"Elizabeth."

Chapter Thirty Two

The Funeral

It was the biggest and most impressive funeral Hamilton City had ever seen. Thousands of people from all walks of life lined the sidewalks leading to the City Park. They were there to honor the man who had worked tirelessly to make Hamilton City the second safest city in the nation. He was the advocate who had chosen reconciliation and accommodation over hostility and confrontation.

The cortege was led by a motorcycle escort. Behind them came the hearse and the chief mourner's limousine. They were followed by over a hundred squad cars and cruisers from all over the state, their headlights shining, their blue and red lights swirling.

A section of the stands had been reserved for Commander Kwame Jackson and past and present pupils from the school founded by the Chief. Gazing at the casket draped in the Stars and Stripes, Commander Jackson said to his friend, the former gang leader Emilio Ramirez, now a successful businessman, "Our communities have lost their best friend."

With tears in his eyes, Emilio clasped his friend's hand and replied, "Well, bro, we'll carry on his good work. We mustn't let him down."

Senator John O'Donnel, his wife Penny and other officials came from Washington, D.C. Senator O'Donnel was to deliver the eulogy, a tribute to the man who had been his best friend. Sir David Knightley and his son Hugh gazed at the ranks of men and women from all the agencies in the state, a sea of blue and gray uniforms, the badges on their chests glinting in the sun.

He thought how proud Elizabeth would have been to see this stunning spectacle. How those two had loved each other. An enduring passion. The bond between them was unbreakable. He sighed deeply. "Well, they were together again."

As the choir from Timothy's school sang "Amazing Grace," Hugh whispered to his father.

"He must have been a great man."

"Yes son. He was a very great man, an exceptional man."

***

The invited guests were gathered on the terrace and the courtyard waiting for Victoria to return from the crematorium. Many of them wandered around the garden, which was at the peak of its beauty. A long trestle table on the terrace was laden with appetizers, salads, cold chicken, roast beef and pastries prepared by Mrs. Gillespie and Birgit Vincent.

Sir David came up to Daniel.

"My deepest sympathy, Daniel. Hamilton City has lost a leader of exceptional ability."

"Thank you sir, I've also lost a man who was a father to me. He was also my best friend."

Sir David took him by the arm. "There's someone who wants to meet you."

He led Daniel to a knot of people on the far side of the terrace.

"Sarah, here's Daniel."

She turned and Daniel gasped.

Elizabeth! The same heart-shaped face, the blue eyes. The dazzling smile.

"Lady Sarah," he stammered.

She regarded him with amusement.

"Don't you Lady Sarah me, Daniel Wentworth. You don't remember me, do you? But I remember you."

"I, I don't..."

"You came to tea with my mother," she paused. "It was a sad day for us. But I remember clearly how happy she was to see you. She'd often spoken about you. She showed Hugh and me photos of you with all your tennis trophies. I've still got them. Even then I thought you were handsome, but now," she said playfully, "I can see you're even more handsome in your uniform."

She laughed.

"Coming from a military family, the women have always had a soft spot for men in uniform. I tell you what, let's go for a turn around the garden."

As she took his hand, he felt a tremor going through him. It was like holding hands with Elizabeth. They strolled around the garden admiring its beauty. She said, "I'm turning eighteen in two months time, so I'm having a party. Do you think you could come?"

What a question—he'd swim the Atlantic if necessary to be present at her party.

"I've got some vacation time, I'd love to come."

"Good, you'll stay with Alan. I'll give you my telephone number. You can call me any time."

He wrote it down and put it in his pocket.

"Now don't lose it."

"I'll sleep with it under my pillow."

They reached the terrace and she said, "We're leaving tomorrow night. I'd like to take you to lunch tomorrow. Maybe we'll have a picnic. I'll ask the hotel chef to prepare a hamper of delicious food. We'll go across the road from the hotel. There's a small park there. We can talk and get to know each other better."

"That sounds great."

He felt he was dreaming; could this really be happening?

She laughed.

"It's like a movie title, *A Picnic in the Park* starring Daniel Wentworth and Sarah Knightley. You don't have to wear your uniform. You'll look good without it."

Two pink spots appeared on her cheeks.

"Oh dear, that sounded risqué. What I meant was you'd look good in anything."

He burst out laughing. Her personality was so like Elizabeth, the confidence, the sense of humor and that entrancing face.

"Well it looks as though Victoria has arrived. I must go to Father, see you tomorrow."

Reluctantly he released her hand, and as she walked away he thought, I'll see to it that there'll be many more tomorrows. Oh Elizabeth it was as though you are reaching across the years, from the very grave, to present me with the gift of your daughter.

***

Victoria thanked the limousine driver and clasping the urn, crossed the driveway and entered the main garden through an iron gate.

She passed the "hot" border, which lived up to its name, an exhilarating mix of orange oriental poppies, crocosmia, red hot pokers and monarda. Edging the border was a dazzling display of red bedding dahlias.

Two slender columns of upright junipers separated the "hot" border from the cooler adjacent "daisy border": white Shasta daisies and yellow helianthus.

She came to the summerhouse where Timothy had proposed to her, the happiest day of her life. Next to the summerhouse was his favorite rose bed planted with David Austin's English roses.

She went through the wide arch which was festooned with the creamy white climber "Sally Holmes."

Standing on the top step she noticed many of the guests admiring the enormous bed of floribunda roses on the upper level. She smiled recalling Timothy's annoyance with four underperforming roses. She and he reading Elizabeth's notes had come across advice which had made them laugh.

"Don't hesitate to get rid of unsatisfactory plants," she had written. "If they're not paying rent, show them the door with a few choice words to speed them on their way."

Near the property line another group was gathered around the water feature. He'd paid for this using a portion of the money bequeathed by Elizabeth.

Water cascaded down a series of massive boulders, then dropped into a pool.

As she walked across the lawn, she glanced at the mixed bed which Timothy had encouraged her to design and plant. She had chosen different shades of pink as the theme: clouds of cleome, cosmos "Sonata" zinnias and vinca. He had been lavish in his praise at the result. Slender upright junipers divided this "pink magic" bed from the enormous blue and white border.

As she gazed at the stunning display, she clasped the urn more firmly and thought, oh Timothy, my beloved Timothy, how happy we were here. How can I live without you?

Timothy had been inspired by the white garden of Vita Scakville-West at Sissinghurst. However, he had incorporated his own ideas into the design.

Two narrow paths formed an arc leading to the small gazebo. In the semi-circle created by the paths, eight white "Iceberg" roses flourished. A carpet of blue lobelia erinus lay beneath them.

The huge area on either side of the roses were a mass of stately purple and blue delphiniums, purple salvia, liatris and lilac colored nepeta.

Interspersed among the sea of blue were the bell-like flowers of white campanula, large clusters of elegant white snapdragons and masses of white phlox paniculata. Two lavender "Hidcote" anchored the border.

Against the eight foot brick wall, built by the former owners to divide the two properties, he had planted eight clematis, royal "Jackmanii." Their tendrils clung firmly to the chicken wire which was stretched across this section of the wall. This majestic climber was a brilliant backdrop for the blue and white perennials in the front.

Another brass plaque had been installed six feet from Elizabeth's. The inscription read:

"Timothy Bennet

An Exceptional Man

A Great Gardener."

Kneeling, she spread the ashes between the two plaques. She positioned the urn horizontally between them. Breaking off two sprigs of lavender, she placed them on either side of the urn.

With tears streaming down her cheeks, Victoria contemplated the sad tableau. She turned and walked back to the house.

A slight breeze sprang up, lifting some of the ashes. The breeze died down, leaving the lavender partially covered with the ashes.

THE END.

Epilogue

What if Elizabeth had not taken a walk that day? The lives of the various characters would have been very different.

Elizabeth married David; her life was content though unexciting.

Timothy, with his superior intellect and engaging personality, excelled in his career. He married an attractive though dull woman who, after the birth of their two children, became a shrew and a nag. He never entered the world of gardening; his gardening activity was limited to the mowing of his suburban lawn.

Daniel graduated from his high school and went on to become a teacher and tennis coach at the local school.

Victoria completed the computer course, and then returned to her home town and a job at the bank.

Tiffany grew older. Her hopes of ensnaring a rich man diminished. She faced stiff competition from the annual crop of young girls gathered around Randy's Bar. Finally with the big 40 looming, in desperation she married a used car salesman, who though unable to satisfy her craving for jewels and expensive shopping trips, was still able to provide her with a plentiful supply of hair extensions.

But Elizabeth did take a walk that day; a walk which would end in that cul-de-sac where she would meet and fall in love with a handsome police officer.

Should we call it Kismet?